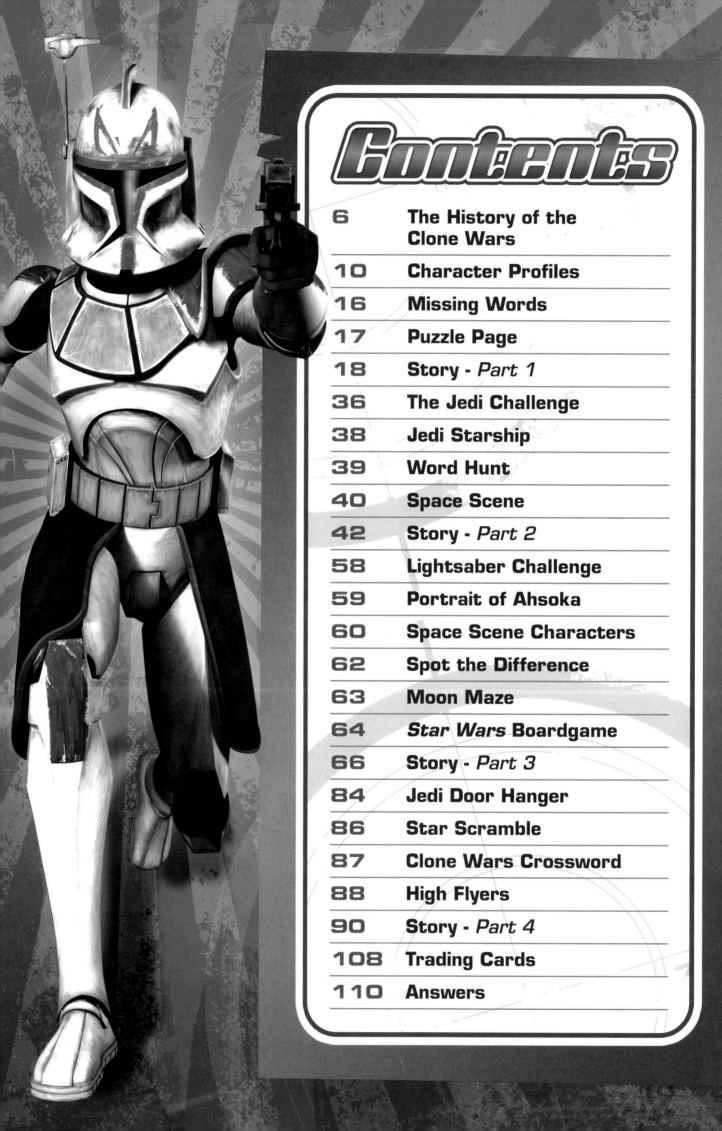

Contents

STAR WARS™

THE CLONE WARS™

£7.99

Pedigree®

Published by Pedigree Books Limited,
Beech Hill House, Walnut Gardens, Exeter, Devon EX4 4DH. Published 2008.

THE HISTORY OF CLONE WARS

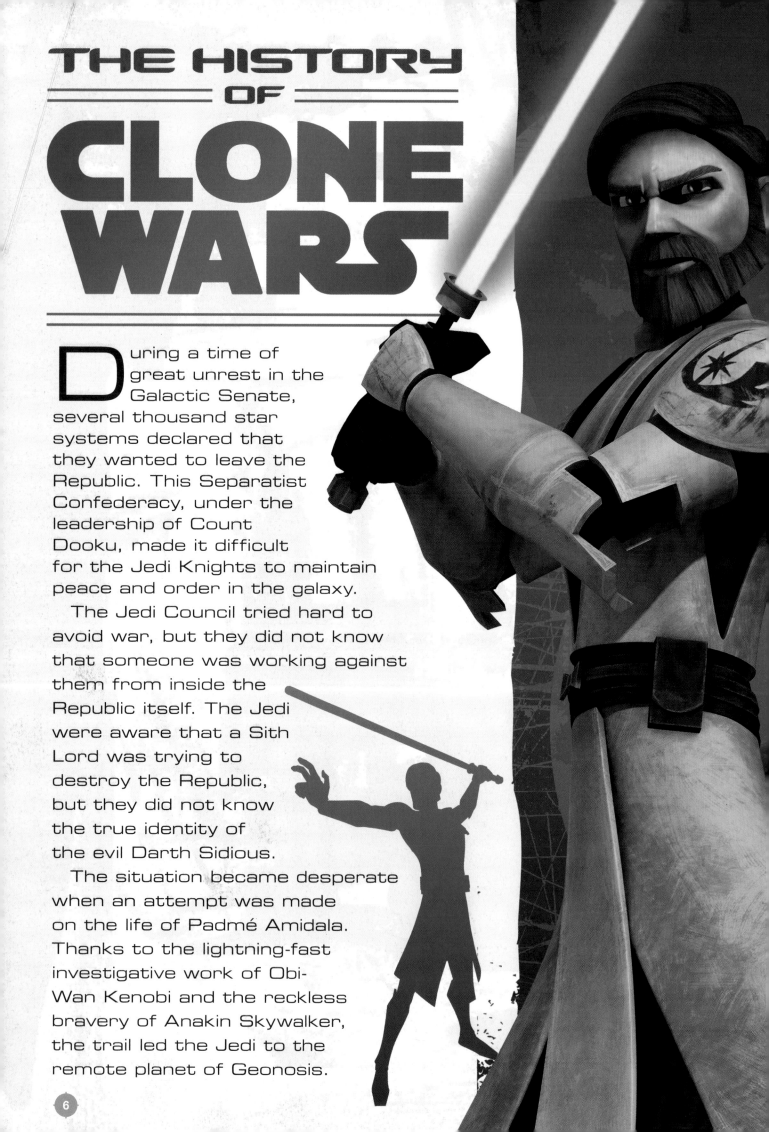

During a time of great unrest in the Galactic Senate, several thousand star systems declared that they wanted to leave the Republic. This Separatist Confederacy, under the leadership of Count Dooku, made it difficult for the Jedi Knights to maintain peace and order in the galaxy.

The Jedi Council tried hard to avoid war, but they did not know that someone was working against them from inside the Republic itself. The Jedi were aware that a Sith Lord was trying to destroy the Republic, but they did not know the true identity of the evil Darth Sidious.

The situation became desperate when an attempt was made on the life of Padmé Amidala. Thanks to the lightning-fast investigative work of Obi-Wan Kenobi and the reckless bravery of Anakin Skywalker, the trail led the Jedi to the remote planet of Geonosis.

Finally, Obi-Wan Kenobi, Padmé Amidala and Anakin Skywalker were captured and condemned to death by the Separatists. At this, the growing conflict between the Republic and the Separatists exploded into full-scale war. For the first time, the clone army of the Republic fought alongside the Jedi against the droid armies of the Confederacy.

THE HISTORY OF CLONE WARS

Following the Battle of Geonosis, the Republic's Jedi Knights led a massive clone army into battles on hundreds of planets. The Separatists, led by the powerful Dark Lords of the Sith, fought back with their own droid armies. As this terrible conflict ripped across the galaxy, Anakin Skywalker, Padmé Amidala and Obi-Wan Kenobi were swept into the turmoil of war and the rising shadow of the dark side.

Jedi Master Yoda devised a strategy of small battles in many locations to gain time for the production of ships, weapons and other war supplies. Jedi secretly infiltrated hundreds of worlds to organise Loyalist resistance, train partisans in sabotage and guerrilla warfare, and do everything they could to destabilise the Separatist movement.

The Clone Wars would produce such heroes as Bail Organa, Anakin Skywalker and General Obi-Wan Kenobi, but not without some devastating losses along the way.

Ahsoka Tano

As a Togruta, Ahsoka Tano has skin the colour of red clay, and white markings around her eyes and on her forehead. Because she is young, the white horns on top of her head are short, and her lekku only just reach her shoulders. One of her head-tails grows down her back and the other two grow down either side of her head. The lekku have alternating stripes of white and bright blue.

Ahsoka was discovered by Master Plo Koon and was raised in the Jedi Temple. As a result of her long Jedi education, she is used to sticking to the rules. She has still to learn that sometimes, a Jedi has to improvise!

Ahsoka is fourteen, two years younger than the usual age when students graduate to Padawan. However, Master Yoda thinks highly of her and has allowed her to graduate early, enabling her to become apprentice to Anakin Skywalker.

Although Ahsoka is proud of her achievement, there is doubt in her mind about whether she truly deserves to be there. She often comforts herself with the thought that Master Yoda believes her to be ready. She doesn't want to fail him. As a result, she is very sensitive to criticism, and is always keen to prove herself.

Most of all, she wants to show her Master what she can do. She is a challenge for Anakin because she is outgoing and independent, just like him!

Anakin Skywalker

Anakin Skywalker is poised to bec[ome] one of the heroes of the Clone War[s]. Although he was once Obi-Wan Kenobi's Padawan, he is now fighting the war as a fully fledged Jedi Knight.

Anakin has many secrets to hide. Against the Jedi code, he has married Padmé Amidala and must conceal his love for her. He must also hide his grief and anger over his mother's death, and the fact that his anger drove him to slaughter the Tusken Raiders who killed her.

The generous, loving boy that Qui-Gon Jinn found on Tatooine has grown into an impetuous and reckless young man. The Force is strong with him, but fear and anger lurk in his heart. Master Yoda assigns the Padawan Ahsoka Tano to Anakin because he is keen to teach the young Jedi a greater sense of responsibility.

Master Obi-Wan Kenobi is an accomplished Jedi, and skilled in Form III lightsaber combat. Although a master of the Jedi lightsaber style known as Ataru, in which deflection is prized above aggression, Obi-Wan's true style is Soresu, which encourages a practitioner to place himself at the eye of the storm. Soresu is well served by Obi-Wan's innate capacity for patience and perception, but the key to mastery is audacity, a talent he has learned from Anakin.

In the years leading up to the start of the Clone Wars, Obi-Wan has developed a wide variety of skills ranging from diplomacy and psychology to military strategy and hand-to-hand combat. He has had to be ready for anything on his field assignments.

Obi-Wan is a wise, kind and courageous Jedi. He is loyal to his friends and has a wry sense of humour that has sustained him through the most dangerous situations.

Obi-Wan Kenobi

Mace Windu

Mace Windu is a senior member of the Jedi Council. He prefers to seek peaceful solutions to problems, so the Clone Wars force him to act against his inner nature. Despite his dislike of violence, Windu is the most fearsome warrior of all the Jedi on the Council. He has complete mastery over Jedi fighting styles. Only two others have ever defeated him in battle – Yoda and Count Dooku.

Master Yoda is the oldest member of the Jedi Council, an expert in Form IV lightsaber combat and a wise and cautious Jedi Master. Many of the Republic's greatest Jedi trained under Yoda when they were children.

Yoda's advice and opinions hold great weight, and he is revered for his wisdom. He has visited hundreds of worlds in his quest to deepen his understanding of the Force. He is thoughtful and deliberate.

Master Yoda

Padmé Amidala

As wise as she was beautiful, Padmé joined the Apprentice Legislature at the age of eleven and was elected Queen of Naboo at the age of fourteen. However, all her self-discipline could not prevent her from falling in love with her Jedi protector, Anakin Skywalker.

C-3PO

C-3PO is a worrisome protocol droid who was built by Anakin Skywalker when he was a boy on Tatooine. C-3PO can be a little stiff and awkward in his manner and he tends to look on the down side. However, he serves Padmé Amidala loyally and he is devoted to the Republic.

R2-D2 is Anakin Skywalker's brave astromech droid, and is a staunch and spirited companion. He is designed to operate in deep space, interfacing with fighter craft and computer systems. He is usually placed in a socket behind the cockpit, where he monitors and diagnoses flight performance, maps and stores hyperspace data, and pinpoints technical errors or faulty computer coding.

R2-D2

Clone Captain Rex
[CC-7567]

Rex is second in command to Anakin Skywalker during the Clone Wars, and he is a freethinking and aggressive soldier's-soldier. Rex is as tough as nails, and is willing to voice his professional opinion to even the highest-ranking Jedi. Rex and his men are assigned to patrol the most lawless and dangerous sectors of the galaxy within the feared Outer Rim.

Supreme Chancellor Palpatine [Darth Sidious]

As Supreme Chancellor, Palpatine has promised to put an end to corruption in the Senate. However, the Republic has only become more chaotic. Now the Separatist movement threatens its fragile unity. The Senate has given Chancellor Palpatine emergency powers and he has ordered the Republic's new clone army into operation.

The Jedi do not know that Palpatine has risen to power through cunning, deception and treachery. As a Sith apprentice he was instructed in the dark side of the Force by Darth Plagueis the Wise. His true intentions are as dark as his heart, and his plans could spell the end of the Jedi Order itself.

Jabba is a Hutt gangster who lives on Tatooine and has collected a fortune through crime. Jabba controls the majority of the planet's cities, towns and spaceports. His empire spans a vast range of criminal activities, including piracy, slavery, gambling and the sale of stolen goods.

The decadence of Jabba's palace attracts the scum of the galaxy, who flock there for drink, food, entertainment and work. Thieves, smugglers, assassins and spies are constantly at Jabba's side. However, he has a great deal of power and both he Republic and the Separatists are keen for him to ally with them.

Jabba the Hutt

Ziro the Hutt

The Hutt crime lord of Coruscant is Jabba the Hutt's uncle, and he is even fatter and more unpleasant than Jabba. He lives in a palace that towers over the streets of downtown Coruscant.

Ziro's palace is decorated inside and out, and he likes to sit in state on a round throne, lit up by different coloured flashing lights. Unlike Jabba, Ziro prefers to speak in the language of the Republic.

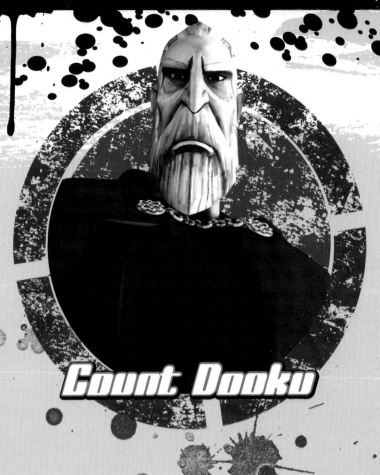

Count Dooku

Count Dooku is a powerful leader and a master swordsman. He was once a respected Jedi, but he turned on the Jedi Order and joined the dark side and the mysterious Darth Sidious.

After Dooku left the Order, he began to encourage rebellion in the galaxy. In a very short time he rallied thousands of systems to his cause, building a growing Separatist movement. He created the Confederacy of Independent Systems, in which representatives from many federations and unions pooled their resources together to form the largest military force in the galaxy. At last, under the orders of Darth Sidious, he started the Clone Wars.

Dooku may look like a frail, elderly man, but he is in fact a fierce warrior. His strength in the Force makes him enigmatic even to Yoda, and the Jedi Council underestimates him at their peril.

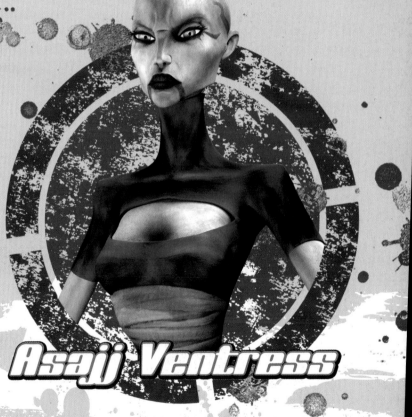

Asajj Ventress

Asajj Ventress is Count Dooku's most trusted assassin. She is not officially a Sith, but she has been trained in the arts of lightsaber duelling and Force manipulation. Her home planet, Rattatak, is a barbaric and violent world.

Shortly after the outbreak of the Clone Wars, Count Dooku came to Rattatak, looking for another world to add to the Separatist Confederacy. Asajj's raw talent and fierce determination impressed him and he invited her to join him.

Though Ventress longs to identify herself as a Sith, she has not received Sith training. Her skills are a combination of incomplete Jedi training and her own techniques. Her anger and pain bolster her dark side abilities. Giving into her rage grants her further powers. Ventress is more than a match for the Republic's greatest Jedi.

MISSING WORDS

Can you complete these fascinating facts by filling in the missing words? Choose the correct words from the box below.

1) Asajj Ventress's fanblade starfighter, *Last Call*, is equipped with a _____ and _____ _____.

2) Anakin's starfighter began as a standard Delta-7 *Aethersprite* that he has customised to suit his need for _____ and control. It has four _____ _____ on each wingtip and a _____ _____ _____ along the ship's dorsal centre line.

3) Jabba's the Hutt's luxury yacht ship has hidden _____ as an unpleasant surprise for would-be pirates.

4) Asajj Ventress uses twin curved, red bladed _____. The handles can connect to form an S-shaped, double-bladed weapon.

5) Each lightsaber is handcrafted as part of a Jedi's training and may have unique design elements. A lightsaber's _____ _____ is produced by several _____ connected to a power source within the lightsaber's handle.

6) Blasters fire beams of intense _____ _____ and the colour of the energy bolts varies. A blaster's gas chamber carries enough blaster gas for over _____ shots. Stun blasts knock the target out for up to _____ minutes, while a _____ _____ _____ can penetrate _____.

7) Jedi are not allowed to _____.

8) Ahsoka's _____ _____ is called R3-G7.

9) Asajj gave Anakin his _____ during a _____ on Coruscant.

10) Anakin Skywalker has earned the title "_____ with no fear" for his exploits in battle.

500
ARMOUR
ASTROMECH DROID
CRYSTALS
DUEL
ENERGY BLADE
FULL POWER BLAST
GEMCUTTER
GUNPORTS
HERO
LASER CANNONS
LIGHT ENERGY
LIGHTSABERS
MARRY
PROTON TORPEDO LAUNCHER
SCAR
SPEED
TEN
TRACTOR BEAMS

PUZZLE PAGE

Tackle these brainteasers to keep your mind alert and active

Riddles

1) What goes around the planet but stays in the corner?

_____

2) What is brown and has a head and a tail, but no legs?

_____

3) If you have me, you want to share me. But if you share me, you haven't got me. What am I?

_____

Anagrams

Can you unscramble these anagrams to figure out the **hidden names**?

1) DREAMY OATS → _____

2) MAMA AIDED PAL → _____

3) PALE PAINT → _____

Conundrums

• A Tusken Raider rides into Mos Eisley on Tuesday. He is tired, so he spends one night at a friend's house. He rides out of Mos Eisley on Tuesday. How does he do it?

_____

• A Padawan turns off the light in his bedroom. The light switch is twenty feet from the bed, but he still manages to get into his bed before it is dark. How does he do it?

_____

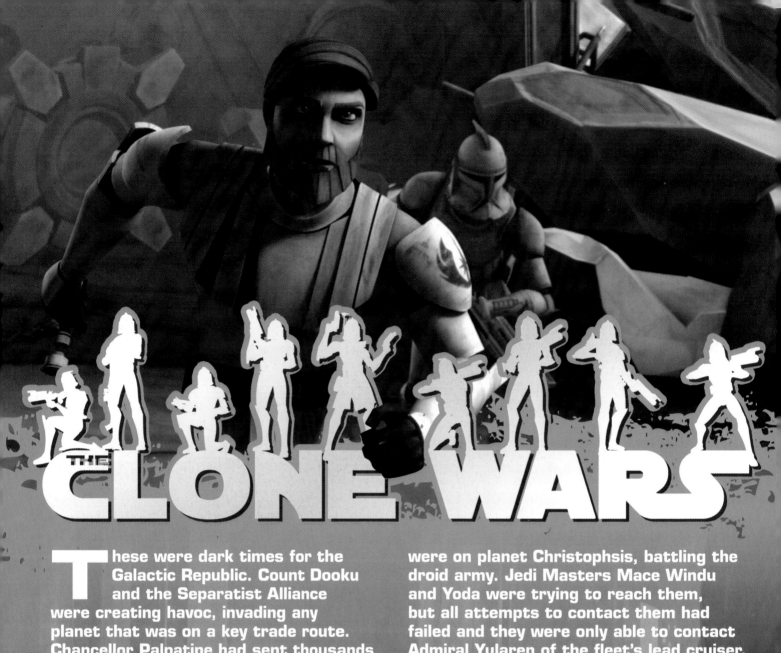

THE CLONE WARS

These were dark times for the Galactic Republic. Count Dooku and the Separatist Alliance were creating havoc, invading any planet that was on a key trade route. Chancellor Palpatine had sent thousands of clone troopers, under the command of the Jedi, to defend the planets.

Obi-Wan Kenobi and Anakin Skywalker were on planet Christophsis, battling the droid army. Jedi Masters Mace Windu and Yoda were trying to reach them, but all attempts to contact them had failed and they were only able to contact Admiral Yularen of the fleet's lead cruiser. They told him that they were sending a messenger with important orders for General Kenobi.

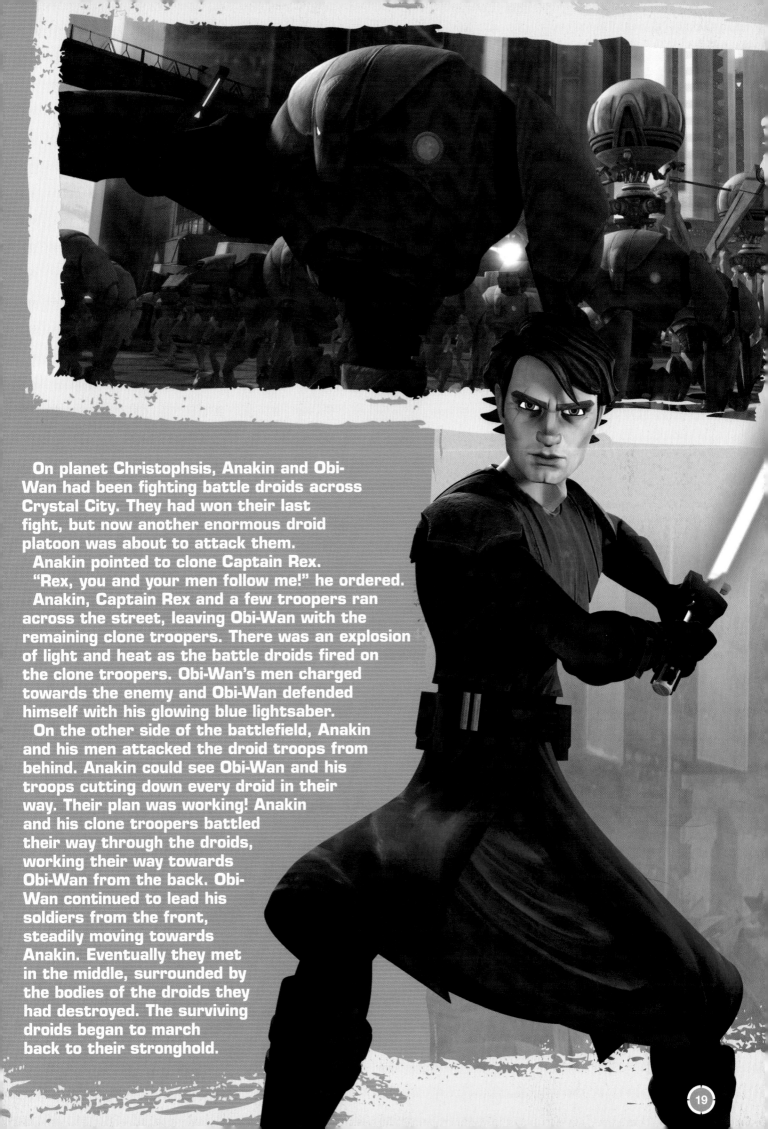

On planet Christophsis, Anakin and Obi-Wan had been fighting battle droids across Crystal City. They had won their last fight, but now another enormous droid platoon was about to attack them.

Anakin pointed to clone Captain Rex.

"Rex, you and your men follow me!" he ordered.

Anakin, Captain Rex and a few troopers ran across the street, leaving Obi-Wan with the remaining clone troopers. There was an explosion of light and heat as the battle droids fired on the clone troopers. Obi-Wan's men charged towards the enemy and Obi-Wan defended himself with his glowing blue lightsaber.

On the other side of the battlefield, Anakin and his men attacked the droid troops from behind. Anakin could see Obi-Wan and his troops cutting down every droid in their way. Their plan was working! Anakin and his clone troopers battled their way through the droids, working their way towards Obi-Wan from the back. Obi-Wan continued to lead his soldiers from the front, steadily moving towards Anakin. Eventually they met in the middle, surrounded by the bodies of the droids they had destroyed. The surviving droids began to march back to their stronghold.

As Anakin and Obi-Wan watched the droids retreat, they noticed something else: a Republic attack shuttle flying high overhead. The elegant, white spacecraft with its red markings was a sight that made both Jedi smile in relief.

"Looks like help has arrived!" Obi-Wan said. "Our cruiser must be back. This solves all our problems. Fresh troops, new supplies, and perhaps they brought my new Padawan with them."

"You really think it's a good idea to bring a Padawan learner into all this?" Anakin asked.

Obi-Wan nodded. "I spoke to Master Yoda about it. You should put in a request for one. You'd make a good teacher."

Anakin chuckled. He felt that he was busy enough fighting in the war, without having to look after a young Padawan who wouldn't know what they were doing.

"No thanks," he said.

Obi-Wan sighed.

"Anakin, teaching is a privilege," he said. "It's part of a Jedi's responsibility to help teach the next generation."

"A Padawan would just slow me down," Anakin replied.

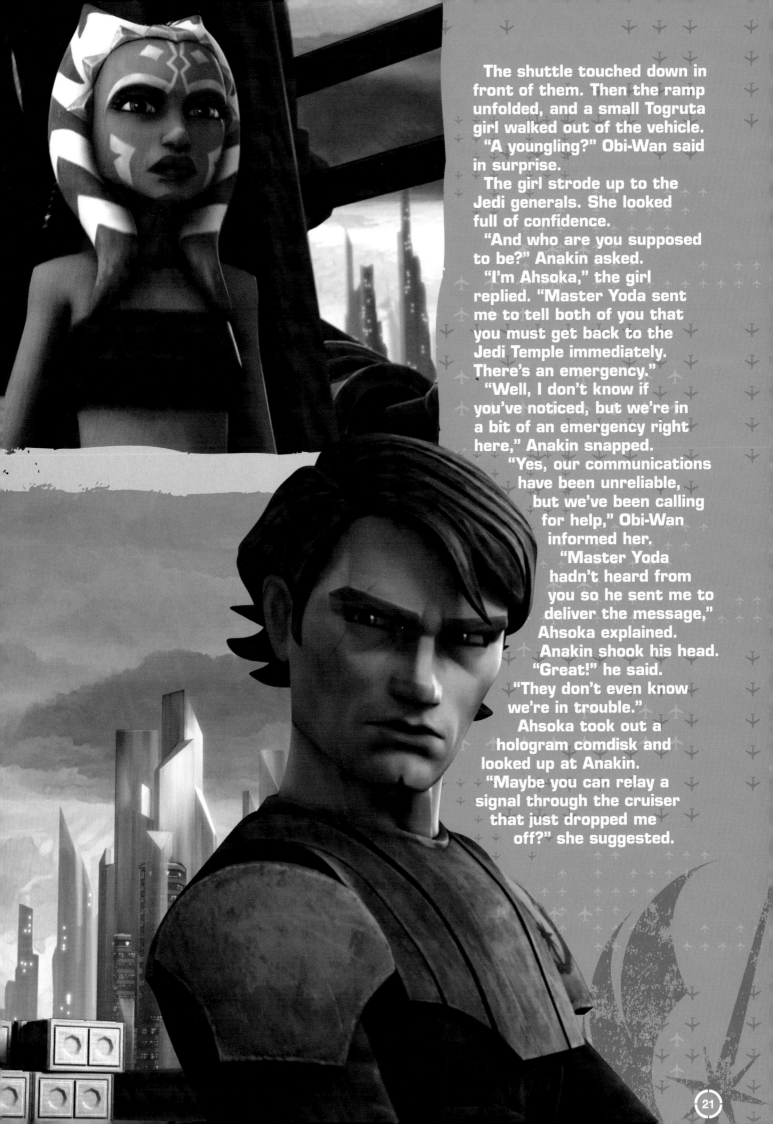

The shuttle touched down in front of them. Then the ramp unfolded, and a small Togruta girl walked out of the vehicle.

"A youngling?" Obi-Wan said in surprise.

The girl strode up to the Jedi generals. She looked full of confidence.

"And who are you supposed to be?" Anakin asked.

"I'm Ahsoka," the girl replied. "Master Yoda sent me to tell both of you that you must get back to the Jedi Temple immediately. There's an emergency."

"Well, I don't know if you've noticed, but we're in a bit of an emergency right here," Anakin snapped.

"Yes, our communications have been unreliable, but we've been calling for help," Obi-Wan informed her.

"Master Yoda hadn't heard from you so he sent me to deliver the message," Ahsoka explained.

Anakin shook his head. "Great!" he said.

"They don't even know we're in trouble."

Ahsoka took out a hologram comdisk and looked up at Anakin.

"Maybe you can relay a signal through the cruiser that just dropped me off?" she suggested.

21

They managed to communicate with Yoda long enough to ask for reinforcements, but then the transmission failed. The cruiser had to leave orbit to avoid enemy ships.

Anakin sighed. "I guess we'll have to hold out a little longer."

Obi-Wan turned to Ahsoka. "It's time for a proper introduction," he said.

"I'm the new Padawan learner, Ahsoka Tano," the girl replied.

"I'm Obi-Wan Kenobi, your new Master," said Obi-Wan with a welcoming smile.

"I'm at your service, Master Kenobi," said Ahsoka with the greatest respect, "but I've actually been assigned to Master Skywalker."

"What?" cried Anakin. "No, no, no! There must be some mistake. He's the one who wanted the Padawan."

"Master Yoda was very specific," Ahsoka said. "I am assigned to Anakin Skywalker and he is to supervise my Jedi training."

Obi-Wan interrupted before Anakin could start yelling again.

"We'll have to sort this out later," he said. "It won't be long before those droids figure out a way around our cannons."

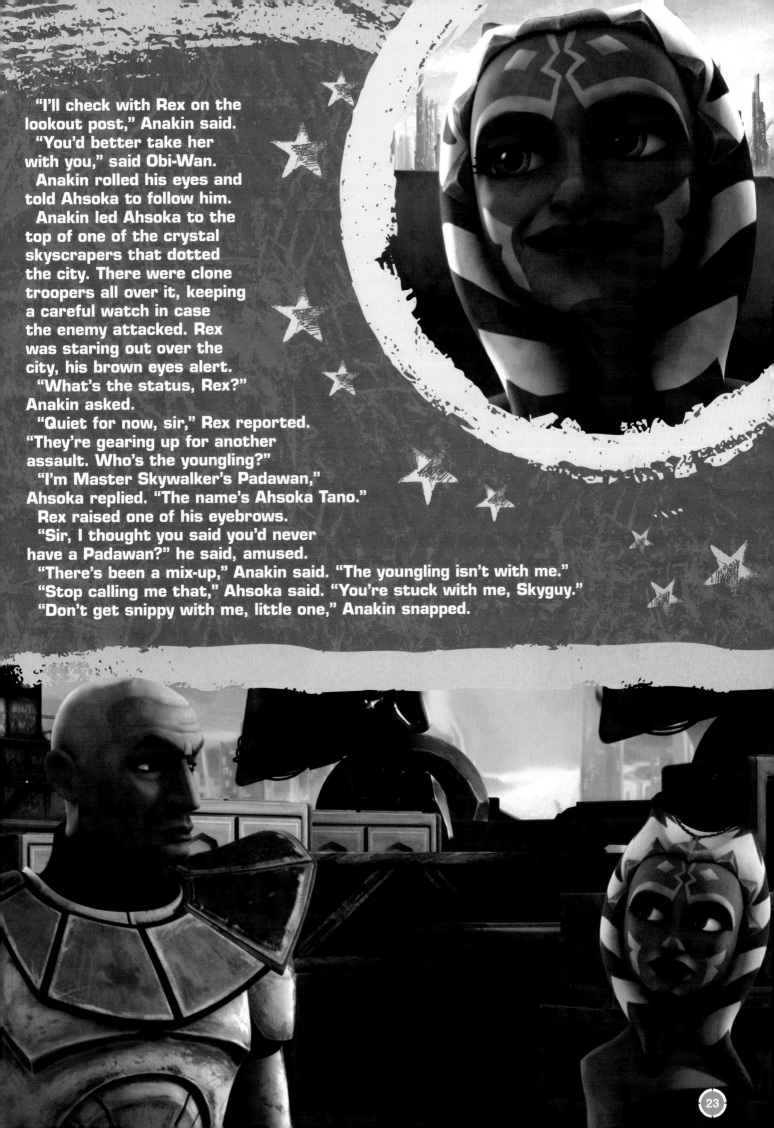

"I'll check with Rex on the lookout post," Anakin said.

"You'd better take her with you," said Obi-Wan.

Anakin rolled his eyes and told Ahsoka to follow him.

Anakin led Ahsoka to the top of one of the crystal skyscrapers that dotted the city. There were clone troopers all over it, keeping a careful watch in case the enemy attacked. Rex was staring out over the city, his brown eyes alert.

"What's the status, Rex?" Anakin asked.

"Quiet for now, sir," Rex reported. "They're gearing up for another assault. Who's the youngling?"

"I'm Master Skywalker's Padawan," Ahsoka replied. "The name's Ahsoka Tano."

Rex raised one of his eyebrows.

"Sir, I thought you said you'd never have a Padawan?" he said, amused.

"There's been a mix-up," Anakin said. "The youngling isn't with me."

"Stop calling me that," Ahsoka said. "You're stuck with me, Skyguy."

"Don't get snippy with me, little one," Anakin snapped.

Anakin sent Ahsoka to check on the troops with Captain Rex. Just as Ahsoka was saying that she hoped to gain some experience, a giant, glowing dome of orange-red energy appeared on the other edge of the city.

"What's that?" Ahsoka asked.

"Not good," Rex said. "They've got an energy shield. It'll be nearly impossible to hold back their attack."

At that moment, the dome started to grow larger. Slowly but surely, it was getting closer to the centre of the city.

"If you want experience, little one, it looks like you're about to get plenty," Rex said.

A few minutes later, Anakin, Obi-Wan, Rex and Ahsoka were huddling together inside the communication station, poring over a large map of the city.

"The shield generator's somewhere in here," said Obi-Wan, pointing to a spot on the map. "They're slowly increasing the size of the energy shield, and keeping it just ahead of their troops."

"Artillery's going to be useless against that," Rex said.

"If that shield's going to be such a problem, why don't we just take it out?" Ahsoka asked.

"Easier said than done," Rex told her.

"I agree with her," Anakin said.

Everyone looked at Anakin in surprise.

"Someone has to get to that shield generator and destroy it," Anakin went on. "That's the key."

"Right, then," Obi-Wan agreed. "Maybe you two can tiptoe through enemy lines and solve this particular problem together."

Despite the danger, Ahsoka felt wildly happy and excited. She was actually going to be part of a Jedi mission at last! Obi-Wan examined the map again and pointed to a different place.

"If Rex and I can engage them *here*, you two might have a chance to get through their lines, undetected, *there*," he said.

"We'll figure out a way!" Ahsoka said. "Come on, Master, let's go!"

"If we survive this, Snips, you and I are going to have a talk," Anakin replied.

Anakin and Ahsoka left the communication station and looked into the distance. The massive droid army was heading steadily towards them, protected by the glowing energy shield.

"So, what's the plan?" Ahsoka asked.

"Oh, I thought *you* were the one with the plan," said Anakin with deep sarcasm.

"No, *I'm* the one with the enthusiasm," the Padawan replied. "You're the one with the experience, which I'm looking forward to learning from."

"Well, first we need to get behind that shield, then get behind their tank lines," Anakin said.

"Why don't we just go around the shield?" Ahsoka asked.

"That'd take too long," Anakin replied.

"Sneak through the middle, then?" Ahsoka suggested.

"Impossible. Unless you want to turn yourself into a droid."

"All right, you win!" said Ahsoka, holding up her hands. "My first lesson will be to wait while you come up with the answer."

Anakin gave a sudden smile. Ahsoka had given him an idea. He had seen a piece of rubble that looked like a big trunk.

He and Ahsoka crawled beneath it, so that it covered them completely. Then they crawled towards the droid army on their hands and knees. It was slow work, and Anakin was slowed down by the satchel around his neck; it contained the explosives they would need to destroy the shield.

"This is a stupid plan!" Ahsoka grumbled eventually. "We should fight these guys instead of sneaking around."

"My stupid plan is working," Anakin replied. "We passed under the shield some time ago, without being detected."

Suddenly there was a low rumbling sound and the ground started to shake. Anakin lifted the trunk and they gasped in horror. The street in front of them was packed with Corporate Alliance tank droids. They were going to be trampled to death!

"Get out, quick!" Anakin bellowed.

He grabbed Ahsoka and together they stumbled and ran out of the way. Anakin pulled the trunk over them both again. Ahsoka's heart thumped so loud she thought everyone must be able to hear it. They had survived, but it had been a by a narrow squeak.

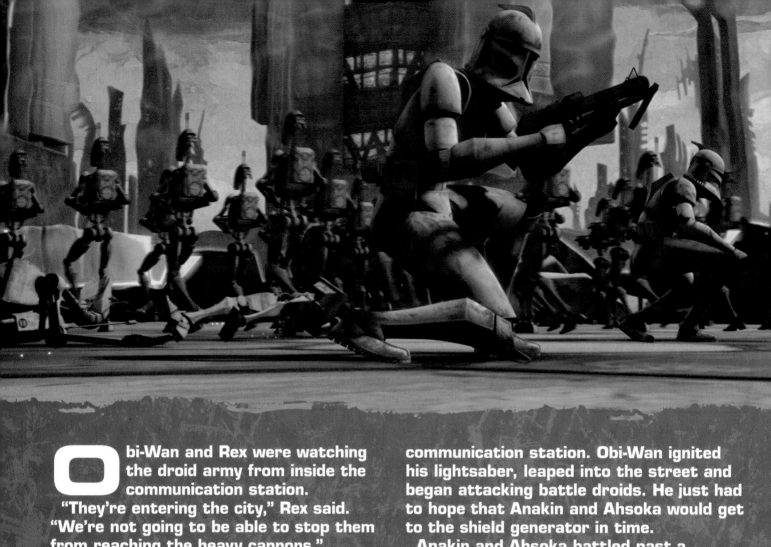

Obi-Wan and Rex were watching the droid army from inside the communication station.

"They're entering the city," Rex said. "We're not going to be able to stop them from reaching the heavy cannons."

"Move your troops back to the cannons," Obi-Wan said. "Do everything you can do to protect them. I'll delay the droids."

Rex led his troops away from the communication station. Obi-Wan ignited his lightsaber, leaped into the street and began attacking battle droids. He just had to hope that Anakin and Ahsoka would get to the shield generator in time.

Anakin and Ahsoka battled past a destroyer droid and soon came to an open field littered with the shells of bombed-out buildings. A shield generator was standing in the centre of the field.

"There it is!" Ahsoka cried. "Come on!"

"Stay close," Anakin instructed. "We've got to be careful."

But Ahsoka ignored him.

"We're almost there!" she cried.

"I said *wait*!" Anakin yelled.

Because she was rushing, Ahsoka triggered a loud alarm and a hidden army of droids began to appear.

"Oops," Ahsoka said.

"Forget about the droids," Anakin said, throwing her the satchel and preparing to fight. "Set the charges!"

Back at the communication station, Obi-Wan was fighting with skill and strength, and he destroyed many droids. But in the end there were just too many for him to overcome. A giant tank rolled towards him and stopped. Then General Loathsom's big blue head appeared out of the hatch.

"You must be the infamous General Kenobi," Loathsom said.

"I surrender!" said Obi-Wan, raising his hands in the air.

The General climbed out of the tank as a battle droid took Obi-Wan's lightsaber. Obi-Wan thought fast. Loathsom was known for being vain and cruel. Perhaps he could use that to his advantage.

Obi-Wan sat at a table and asked General Loathsom to sit down too. He had to stall him for as long as possible.

"It's a rare honour to be able to meet one's opponent face-to-face," Obi-Wan said. "You're a legend throughout the Inner Core."

"Thank you," Loathsom said, beaming. "The honour is all mine. I'm glad you decided to surrender rather than to fight this out to the bitter end."

"Well, at some point, we must accept the reality of the situation," Obi-Wan said. "Might we have some refreshments?"

Anakin fought off the droids while Ahsoka raced around as fast as she could, sticking explosive charges to the shield generator. Finally she put the last one on the control panel and then turned it on. All the charges started to flash and beep. Then she ignited her lightsaber and ran away from the shield generator to join Anakin. The droids had backed her Master up against a tall, crumbling wall. Ahsoka looked up and saw an open window in the wall.

"Skyguy, don't move!" she called out.

"What?" Anakin replied, going pale as he realised what she was going to do.

"No, no, no!"
Ahsoka focused on the wall and used the Force to bring it crumbling down, smashing the droids to pieces underneath it. Anakin was perfectly safe, just as Ahsoka had planned. The window had fallen around him.

Obi-Wan was sipping a cup of tea.
"Once you've taken custody of my troops, arrangements will need to be made for their food and shelter," he said. "Tell me, do you have enough supplies to –"
"Enough of this!" Loathsom fumed, pounding a clawed fist on the table. "You are stalling!"
"Nonsense!" Obi-Wan replied. "General, there are numerous details to discuss."

Loathsom growled and stood up. "Seize him!" he ordered.

Obi-Wan realised that he would stand for no more stalling. He leaped into the air and jumped over the droids. He landed behind them and used the power of the Force to smash them into each other. As fast as lightning, Obi-Wan raced behind General Loathsom and grabbed him around his revolting neck so that he could not move. The droids had been about to shoot him, but now they paused, not daring to risk killing their general.

By the field, Ahsoka pressed the detonator and the charges exploded, blowing up the generator. The orange dome that was protecting the troops shuddered and then vanished. Obi-Wan gave a wide grin as he realised that Anakin and Ahsoka had succeeded.

"Something appears to have happened to your shield, General," he said.

Loathsom slumped in despair as a hologram image of Admiral Yularen flickered on to the screen in front of them.

"General Kenobi, we're through the blockade," he reported. "The Separatist armada is in retreat. Your reinforcements should be landing in a moment."

Obi-Wan could see Republic cruisers and fighters landing in the distance.

"It's all over now, General," Obi-Wan told Loathsom, without releasing his grip. "Now it's my turn to negotiate the treaty. Tell your troops to lay down their arms."

"Surrender! Surrender!" Loathsom cried.

Now that the danger was over, Ahsoka felt weak with relief. She sat down in the field as she realised how close to death she had come in the last hour. Anakin sat down beside her.

"You're reckless, little one," he said. "You would never have made it as Obi-Wan's Padawan, but you might make it as mine."

Ahsoka could hardly believe her ears. She had felt sure that Anakin would be sending her back to Coruscant as soon as he could. As she realised that he wanted to keep her with him, a grin spread across her face. Anakin smiled back at her. Then they heard the whir of a spacecraft and a Jedi gunship landed next to them. Help had arrived.

The spacecraft flew into orbit and docked on a Jedi cruiser. Anakin and Ahsoka left the cruiser and saw Obi-Wan and Yoda waiting for them. Anakin and Ahsoka bowed to the two Jedi Masters.

"Trouble you have with your new Padawan, I hear," said Yoda. "If not ready for a Padawan you are, then perhaps Obi-Wan can . . ."

"Now wait a minute!" Anakin interrupted. "I admit Ahsoka's a little rough around the edges. But with a great deal of training and patience, she might amount to something."

Yoda and Obi-Wan glanced at each other, looking pleased.

"Then go with you, she will, to the Teth system," Yoda said. "Kidnapped, Jabba the Hutt's son has been."

"You want me to rescue Jabba's son?" asked Anakin in amazement.

"We'll need the Hutt's allegiance to give us an advantage over Dooku," Obi-Wan said.

"Negotiate the treaty with Jabba, Obi-Wan will," Yoda instructed. "Find the renegades that hold Jabba's son your mission will be, Skywalker,"

"Come on, Master, it doesn't sound that hard," Ahsoka urged. "I'll find Rex and get the troops organised."

The Jedi watched her as she hurried away to look for Rex.

"Don't worry, Anakin," Obi-Wan said. "Just teach her everything I taught you and she'll turn out fine."

"You know, something makes me think this was your idea from the start," Anakin said.

Obi-Wan's eyes twinkled and Anakin knew that he had guessed correctly. Anakin grinned as he said goodbye and boarded his gunship. From now on, he would have the help, and the hindrance, of a new Padawan.

THE JEDI

A Jedi needs powers of deduction as well as combat skills. Complete these Sudoku puzzles to test your detective abilities!

Fill in all the empty squares so that every row, every column and every mini 3x3 column contains each of the numbers 1 to 9.

YOUNGLING LEVEL

		5	6		4	2		
6				8				9
			7		1			
5		4		1		8		2
	3		8		5		1	
9		1		2		7		3
			3		9			
4				5				1
		9	1			7	5	

PADAWAN LEVEL

	2		8		4			6
			1		7			
4	9			2				
3	6						4	1
		8				3		
9	5						6	2
			3				2	8
			9		2			
1			7		8		5	

CHALLENGE

KNIGHT LEVEL

	9			3			8	
		4		5	9			
5	8		9				7	6
	2				6			
7			1					9
		6					3	
8	3			4			1	2
	2		1			5		
	1			9			6	

MASTER LEVEL

		4	8	9				3
	7			5				
					6			9
3			2				7	8
			6		8			
				7			9	
			1					2
			3			8		
1		5		4				

Jedi starship

Use this grid to draw your own image of Anakin's Jedi starfighter. Finish your drawing by adding colour and the Jedi symbols.

Word Hunt

Test your Jedi skills of observation and try to locate the 15 words that are hidden in this grid. Be alert! The words may be forwards, backwards, across, up or diagonal!

Jedi
Separatists
Sith
Dooku
Grievous
Windu
Yoda
Anakin
Ahsoka
Palpatine
Kenobi
Coruscant
Blaster
Droid
Jabba

```
P T U J M N B V C W T N A C S U R O C P
K L U V C E W U I O C Z M T A P Y I Z S
I E N T X W Q T O L K N S B F V I R T R
C N M P R D G W J E D I L H N B C A W T
O I O A S R T U I B T V X M B N L J K V
R T D X A J F R K A I A K O S H A O H G
C A W R T Y L J R H O Y R S U D F G B L
M P V S E I C A Y Q W T V L O K J M L U
R L Y T C V P J L D A U W P V W U N A V
A A E X I E Y R T W R B D R E J Z G S H
X P G N S I T H Y S M O L X I Z I N T Q
U K H A D H V C I R O W I O R L M K E Z
D J H K F V M O U K W S R D G K C I R T
O I A B S I C V U J G L H D P I U O K R
A H X B O T I H D L K O W C V B P O I R
N L V A B Y Q X K L O V I W H O G Z R A
A J L V X A R L V A T K P Q P N A H J D
K F X B M Z U D N I W Y I E J E L G R O
I Y B J A W O Q L K S J U I V K L C V Y
N P Z L J G D O R W V I G K L F E V I O
```

39

SPACE SCENE

Follow the instructions to create your own space scene. Later you will learn how to make characters to stand in your scene!

YOU WILL NEED:

2 SHOEBOXES OR 1 LARGER BOX
THICK TAPE
COLOURED CRAFT PAPER
SILVER FOIL
OLD SPONGE
SCISSORS (ASK A GROWN-UP TO GIVE YOU A HAND WHEN YOU ARE CUTTING OUT)
CRAYONS OR COLOURED PENCILS
PAINT
GLUE
EARBUDS

INSTRUCTIONS:

1. Cut out one long side of each shoebox and then tape the boxes together to make one larger box. Stand the box on one edge so you are facing the bottom of the box.

2. Cut out some tiny star shapes from the foil.

3. Glue two pieces of black paper together and stick the stars on them.

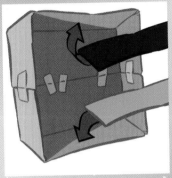

4. Use your crayons or coloured pencils to add in more detail, such as distant planets and maybe a meteor storm!

5. Draw some planets and starships on white paper and colour them in, then stick them to the black background.

6. Stick a piece of black paper to the top part of the inside of the box.

7. Now stick a piece of green paper to the bottom of the box. This is the planet that your characters will land on.

8. Stick the background into the shoebox. Give it a curve when you put it in, to give a more realistic feeling.

9. Cut out some small pieces of sponge and use your paint to colour them. These will be the plants or rocks on the planet, so they can be any colour and shape you like!

10. Glue the pieces of sponge to the green base.

11. Scrunch up some small pieces of coloured paper and add them to the base to add depth and texture to your scene. You could even add real grass, pebbles or moss to help bring your planet to life!

Hutt Castle, the home of vile crime lord Jabba the Hutt, was the tallest building on the planet Tatooine. It was not a pleasant place, but Obi-Wan was there because he had a job to do. Master Yoda had sent him to negotiate a treaty between Jabba and the Republic. He and Jabba had finally agreed that if the Jedi could find Jabba's kidnapped son, Rotta, Jabba would grant the Republic safe passage through Hutt Space.

The Jedi had discovered that Rotta was being held captive on planet Teth, a world in the Outer Rim. Anakin and Ahsoka, together with Rex and a small army of clone troopers, had taken five gunships aboard a Jedi transport and set off for Teth.

Far away from Tatooine, the five gunships were zooming down to the planet surface. Ahsoka peered out. In the distance, she could see a tall palace on top of a high rock. It was an abandoned Hutt castle, and it was the place where Rotta was being held. They had to get inside the castle, rescue Rotta and take him home to Tatooine.

As soon as the ship landed, they were attacked by battle droids! The droids fired on them from the top of the rock. Ahsoka ignited her lightsaber and blocked the laser fire. She could see a line of battle droids on top of the rock. They had to get up there!

"Race you to the top!" Anakin grinned.

"I'll give you a head start," Ahsoka said.

Anakin grabbed a vine and started to climb up the side of the rock. The clone troopers fired suspension cables and attached grappling hooks to the top of the rock wall. They all started to climb up the steep rock, avoiding the blaster fire from the droids as best they could.

"I'm right behind you, Master!" Ahsoka called.

Ahsoka was climbing up the wall using a vine when an **AT-TE** walker passed her. Ahsoka hitched a ride on the back of the walker, using her lightsaber to block the laser fire that bore down on her from above. Then four battle droids on **STAP** fighters came flying along the wall. They aimed for Ahsoka's walker and fired at its feet. The AT-TE lost its grip and Ahsoka fell off the side!

Ahsoka managed to hang on to the walker with one hand, but it was staggering and she couldn't get her balance. The **STAP** fighters swung back around, ready to destroy her. Then Anakin saw what was happening. He jumped on top of the walker and then flipped into the air, destroying two **STAPs** single-handed. Then he leaped onto the third STAP, kicked off the droid pilot and steered it up the rock wall, blasting more droids as he went.

Ahsoka climbed back on top of the walker. Anakin blasted his way up the wall, clearing a path for Rex and the troopers. But when he reached the top, a group of battle droids surrounded him. Anakin slashed through the crowd of droids, but then three destroyer droids rolled up.

"Blast it, Ahsoka," Anakin muttered. "I told you to stay close to me."

The destroyer droids prepared to attack. Then a blast of laser power exploded the droids into pieces. Anakin turned and saw Ahsoka controlling the guns of the AT-TE walker.

"I can't get much closer, Skyguy," Ahsoka said.

Anakin smiled up at her. "I knew you'd get here, Snips, eventually."

"Always in time to save your life," Ahsoka teased.

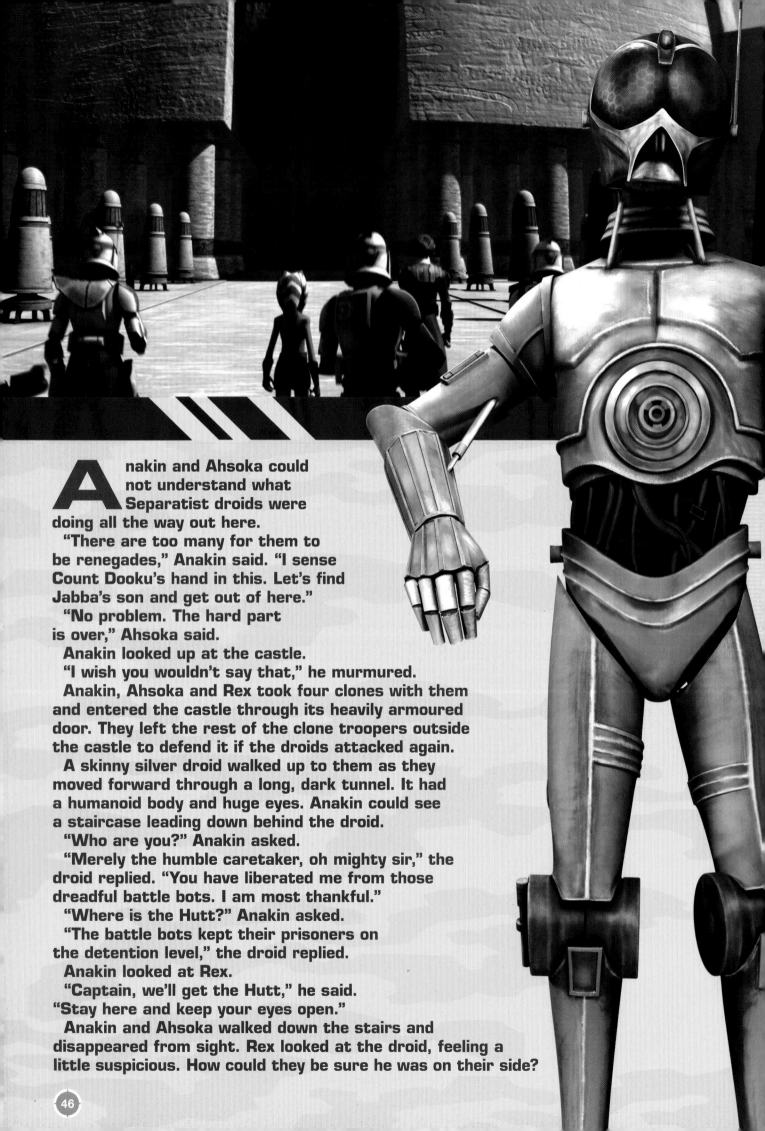

Anakin and Ahsoka could not understand what Separatist droids were doing all the way out here.

"There are too many for them to be renegades," Anakin said. "I sense Count Dooku's hand in this. Let's find Jabba's son and get out of here."

"No problem. The hard part is over," Ahsoka said.

Anakin looked up at the castle.

"I wish you wouldn't say that," he murmured.

Anakin, Ahsoka and Rex took four clones with them and entered the castle through its heavily armoured door. They left the rest of the clone troopers outside the castle to defend it if the droids attacked again.

A skinny silver droid walked up to them as they moved forward through a long, dark tunnel. It had a humanoid body and huge eyes. Anakin could see a staircase leading down behind the droid.

"Who are you?" Anakin asked.

"Merely the humble caretaker, oh mighty sir," the droid replied. "You have liberated me from those dreadful battle bots. I am most thankful."

"Where is the Hutt?" Anakin asked.

"The battle bots kept their prisoners on the detention level," the droid replied.

Anakin looked at Rex.

"Captain, we'll get the Hutt," he said. "Stay here and keep your eyes open."

Anakin and Ahsoka walked down the stairs and disappeared from sight. Rex looked at the droid, feeling a little suspicious. How could they be sure he was on their side?

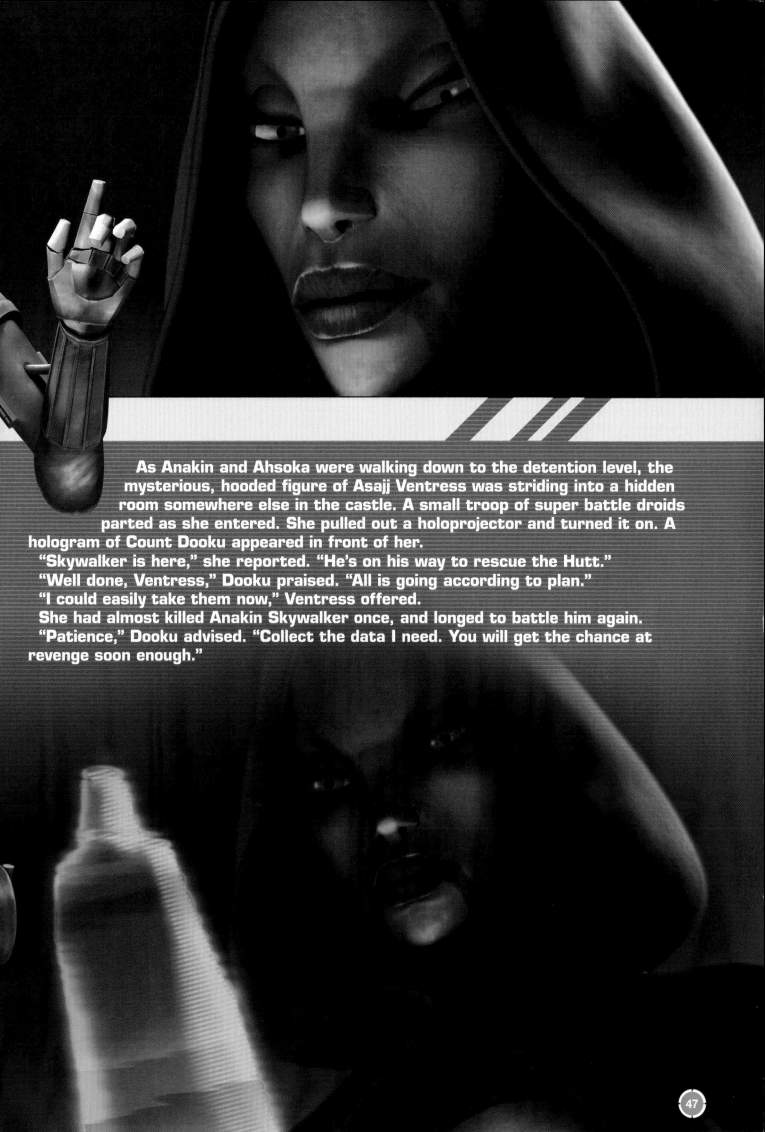

As Anakin and Ahsoka were walking down to the detention level, the mysterious, hooded figure of Asajj Ventress was striding into a hidden room somewhere else in the castle. A small troop of super battle droids parted as she entered. She pulled out a holoprojector and turned it on. A hologram of Count Dooku appeared in front of her.

"Skywalker is here," she reported. "He's on his way to rescue the Hutt."

"Well done, Ventress," Dooku praised. "All is going according to plan."

"I could easily take them now," Ventress offered.

She had almost killed Anakin Skywalker once, and longed to battle him again.

"Patience," Dooku advised. "Collect the data I need. You will get the chance at revenge soon enough."

Anakin and Ahsoka found themselves in a series of winding corridors deep in the dungeons of the castle. As they walked towards one of the cells, Anakin felt his Force senses guiding him.

"I sense our kidnapped Hutt is in here," he said.

Ahsoka pulled a disgusted face.

"Ew . . . I smell him, too!" she exclaimed.

Anakin opened the door of the cell. Inside, sitting miserably on the cold dungeon floor, was a tiny version of Jabba. It was Rotta. He was no taller than Ahsoka's knee. When he saw Anakin and Ahsoka, he started to cry.

"He's a lot younger than I thought he'd be," Anakin said.

"He's just a baby," replied Ahsoka. "This will make our job a lot easier."

Ahsoka knelt down next to Rotta as Anakin activated his comlink.

"We've got Jabba's son, Rex," he said. "Any sign of General Kenobi yet?"

"No, sir," Rex answered.

Ahsoka picked up the slimy Rotta, trying not to let him slip through her arms. He was a lot heavier than he looked. She clung on to his slippery skin and started back to where Rex and the clone troopers were waiting for them. Then they raced back to the main entrance and stepped outside into the castle courtyard.

Anakin stopped and Rotta coughed. Ahsoka felt his forehead. The baby felt very hot.

"Master, I think this little guy is sick," Ahsoka said.

Anakin knelt down and examined the tiny Hutt. His eyes were watery, and his tongue was slimy. Anakin knew that these were not good signs.

"You're right," he said. "We've got to get him back to the ship!"

A trooper brought them a rucksack and they started to put Rotta into it. The baby didn't want to go in, though, and he cried and wriggled, making it very difficult for them to hold on to him.

"I hate Hutts," Anakin grumbled.

Anakin was too busy with Rotta to notice Asajj Ventress. She was hidden in the shadows of the courtyard and the silver droid was next to her, recording everything.

On planet Tatooine, Count Dooku was in Jabba the Hutt's throne room.

"Oh great Jabba the Hutt, I have news of your son," he said. "I have discovered that it is the Jedi who have kidnapped him."

Jabba roared with fury as Count Dooku showed him a hologram recording. It showed Ahsoka and Anakin shoving Rotta into the rucksack as the baby sobbed.

"I hate Hutts!" Jabba heard Anakin say.

"My droid army has already initiated a rescue," Count Dooku said. "Rest assured, mighty Jabba, your son will be saved."

TC-70 translated Jabba's reply. "Mighty Jabba wishes to know what you ask in return."

"Perhaps you would consider joining our struggle against the Republic?" said Count Dooku.

Anakin's Delta-7 starfighter landed in the courtyard. R2-D2 was piloting it. He projected a hologram of Obi-Wan in front of Anakin.

"Anakin, did you locate Jabba's son?" Obi-Wan asked.

"We have him, but it looks like the Separatists are behind his abduction," Anakin reported. "This smells like Count Dooku to me."

"I think it's little Stinky you smell," Ahsoka joked.

"I'll bet Dooku is using us to get Jabba to join the Separatists," said Obi-Wan.

"Master Kenobi, we have another problem," Ahsoka added. "This Huttlet is very sick."

"I'm not sure we can get him back to Tatooine alive, Master," Anakin said. "This whole rescue may backfire on us. I still don't think dealing with the Hutts is a good idea."

"Anakin, they control shipping routes in the Outer Rim," Obi-Wan said. "Jabba's cooperation is crucial to the war effort. If you let anything happen to his son, our chances of a treaty with him will disappear."

Suddenly, there was a flash of light in the sky.

"Master, we've got trouble!" Ahsoka shouted.

A Separatist landing ship appeared with squads of vulture droid fighters, ready to attack.

"Defensive positions!" Rex yelled.

"I'll have to call you back, Master," Anakin said. "We're under attack. We could use a little help here."

"I'll get there as soon as I can!" Obi-Wan promised. "Protect the Hutt, Anakin!"

The swarm of vulture fighters attacked. One fighter destroyed Anakin's starfighter with a torpedo and R2 escaped just in time. Anakin, Ahsoka and the clones had to retreat into the castle. They closed the armoured door and stared at each other in shock.

"Captain, we'll stay here until General Kenobi arrives with reinforcements," Anakin told Rex.

"Master, do you honestly think we can hold them off?" cried Ahsoka. "We've got to find a way out of here."

"Our mandate is to protect this Hutt, and that's what we're going to do, Ahsoka," Anakin said sternly.

"Our mandate was to get this Hutt back to Tatooine, and time is running out," Ahsoka reminded him.

Rotta had gone very green. In his heart, Anakin knew that Ahsoka was right. If they waited for Obi-Wan, Rotta might die before they could return him to his father. Jabba's anger would be directed against the Republic.

"I suppose you have a plan?" he asked.

"I think so," she replied. "Artoo willing."

The little droid beeped eagerly. He was always happiest at the centre of the action.

"All right, Snips, I'll trust you on this one," Anakin said. "Captain, hold them here as long as you can."

"Will do, sir!" Rex replied.

Anakin, Ahsoka and R2 turned and raced into the castle. They had to find an escape route before the droid army made it through the armoured door.

Anakin, Ahsoka and R2 dashed into the throne room and R2 rolled over to the hub and plugged himself into the computer.

"If there's a way out of here, Artoo will find it," Ahsoka said.

"Make it quick," Anakin told the droid.

Ahsoka took off the rucksack and put Rotta on the ground. Suddenly an explosion shook the castle.

"That sounded bad," Anakin said.

They guessed that the battle droids had found a way into the castle. Time was running out. Then R2 discovered that there was a landing platform behind the castle.

"A backdoor landing platform!" Ahsoka said.

"We'll call for a gunship when we get there," Anakin said. "Lead the way, Artoo."
Anakin's comlink crackled.
"Anakin, come in," a voice said. "We've held the droids, sir."

Anakin raised his wrist to reply, and then stopped. There was a disturbance in the Force that told him something was wrong.

"We've held the droids, sir," the voice repeated.

"That's not like Rex," said Anakin, shaking his head.

"What is your location?" the voice asked.

"Ventress," Anakin whispered.

"Count Dooku's assassin?" said Ahsoka.

Anakin could sense Ventress's dark energy. He had been close to it once and he would never forget it.

"She's here to kill the Hutt," he said.

Now he could see the whole evil plan. The Jedi would be blamed for Rotta's death, and Jabba would ally himself with Dooku. They had to get out of there!

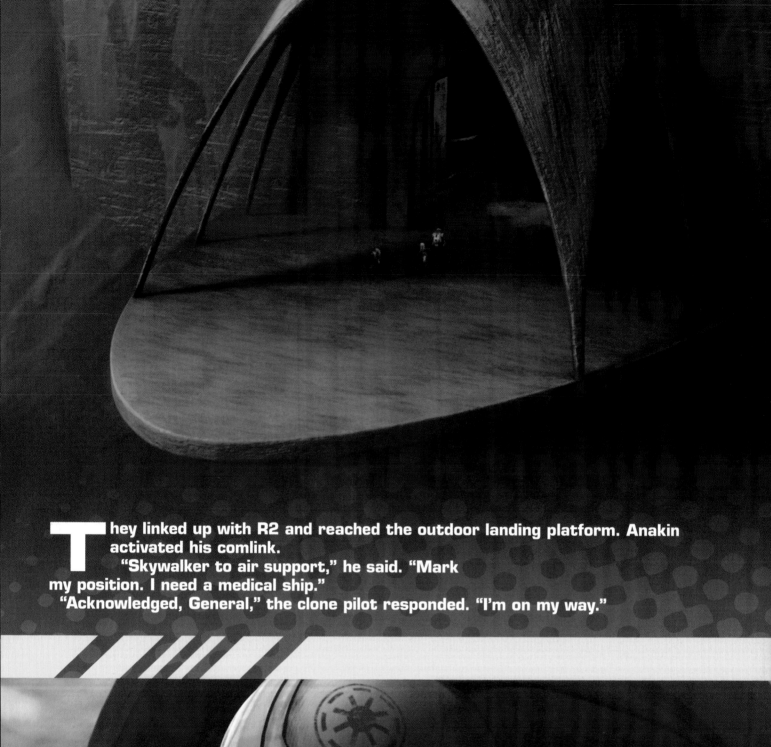

They linked up with R2 and reached the outdoor landing platform. Anakin activated his comlink.

"Skywalker to air support," he said. "Mark my position. I need a medical ship."

"Acknowledged, General," the clone pilot responded. "I'm on my way."

"Ahsoka, you were a great Jedi today," Anakin said.

"Thanks to your instruction, Master," Ahsoka replied, pleased.

She turned to Artoo. "You did a swell job, too, Artoo."

The droid beeped, glad to have been useful.

"You know, Skyguy, that wasn't so difficult after all," Ahsoka said.

But Anakin shook his head.

"We're not out of this yet," he warned her.

Lightsaber Challenge

Asajj Ventress has stolen several lightsabers belonging to her Jedi opponents. Can you return them safely to the Jedi Temple?

Count up how many lightsabers of each colour you can find. Then add them all together to see out how many you have saved!

___ Purple lightsabers.
___ Blue lightsabers.
___ Green lightsabers.
___ Red lightsabers.

I have saved ___ lightsabers!

Portrait
of Ahsoka

Use the grid to draw your own portrait of Anakin's brave new Padawan, Ahsoka Tano.

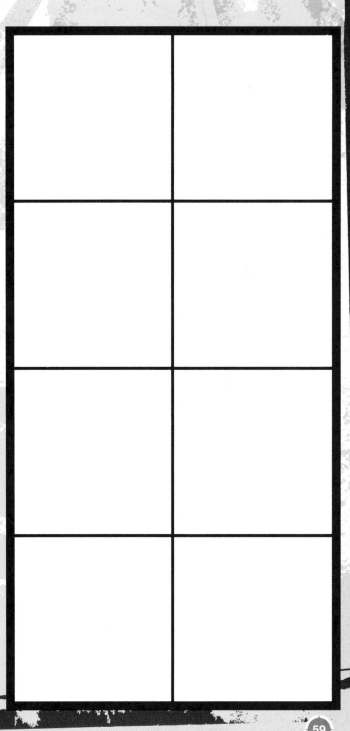

SPACE SCENE CHARACTERS

YOU WILL NEED:

TRACING PAPER
WHITE CARD
COLOURING PENCILS OR CRAYONS
STRING
SCISSORS
GLUE
HOLE PUNCH

INSTRUCTIONS:

1. Use tracing paper to copy the characters on to card.

2. Colour in the characters and the starship. Colour the bases the same shade as the planet.

3. Carefully cut the characters out. Ask a grown-up to help you. Make sure that you don't cut off the bases!

4. Glue your characters into your space scene.

5. Use a hole punch to make a hole at each side of the starship. Make two holes in the roof of your space scene, the same distance apart.

6. Tie two pieces of string through the holes. Push the other ends through the hole in the top of your box, and tie the ends together. You will now have a starship flying through your space scene!

Now it's time to complete the space scene you started earlier!

SPOT THE DIFFERENCE

These two pictures look the same, but there are ten differences. Can you spot them all?

MOON MAZE

Anakin and Ahsoka have been separated on a remote moon, and Asajj Ventress is searching for them! Can you work out how Anakin can reach Ahsoka without bumping into any of their enemies?

Star Wars!

A GAME FOR TWO OR MORE PLAYERS.

Join the Clone Wars and fight alongside Anakin, Ahsoka and Obi-Wan as they try to return Jabba the Hutt's son before the Separatists!

START!

2

3

4

You find Rotta straight away. **TAKE ANOTHER TURN.**

6

7

8

9

28

29

You are separated from your Master. **GO BACK THREE SPACES.**

31

32

33

You are attacked by battle droids. GO BACK TWO SPACES.

YOU WILL NEED:
• A marker for each player
• A dice.

1) Throw the dice to decide who goes first. The player with the highest score starts the game.

2) Throw the dice and move your marker along the squares.

3) Check out the instructions on the square where you land and do what they say!

4) The first player to reach Jabba the Hutt is

27

26

Asajj Ventress blocks your escape route. **LOSE A TURN.**

24

23

22

21

You lose Rotta. **LOSE A TURN.**

19

18

17

16

You contact air support and request a medical ship. **JUMP FORWARD TWO SPACES.**

FINISH!

39

38

37

36

The Separatists have told Jabba his life is in danger! about you and your life is in danger! **SWAP MARKER POSITIONS WITH THE PLAYER ON YOUR RIGHT.**

34

14

13

12

11

65

Rotta squirmed and coughed as a Republic gunship landed on the platform.

"Hang in there, Stinky," said Ahsoka.

Suddenly a shadow passed over them. A vulture droid bomber dived down and bombed the gunship, which exploded in a ball of flame. The blast knocked all of them off their feet. Anakin and Ahsoka leaped up and destroyed the vulture droid, but now they had no transport, and Ventress was not far behind them. Anakin tried to reach Obi-Wan via the comlink, but all transmissions were jammed. Anakin tried to reach Rex. At first there was no reply, but finally he heard the clone captain's voice.

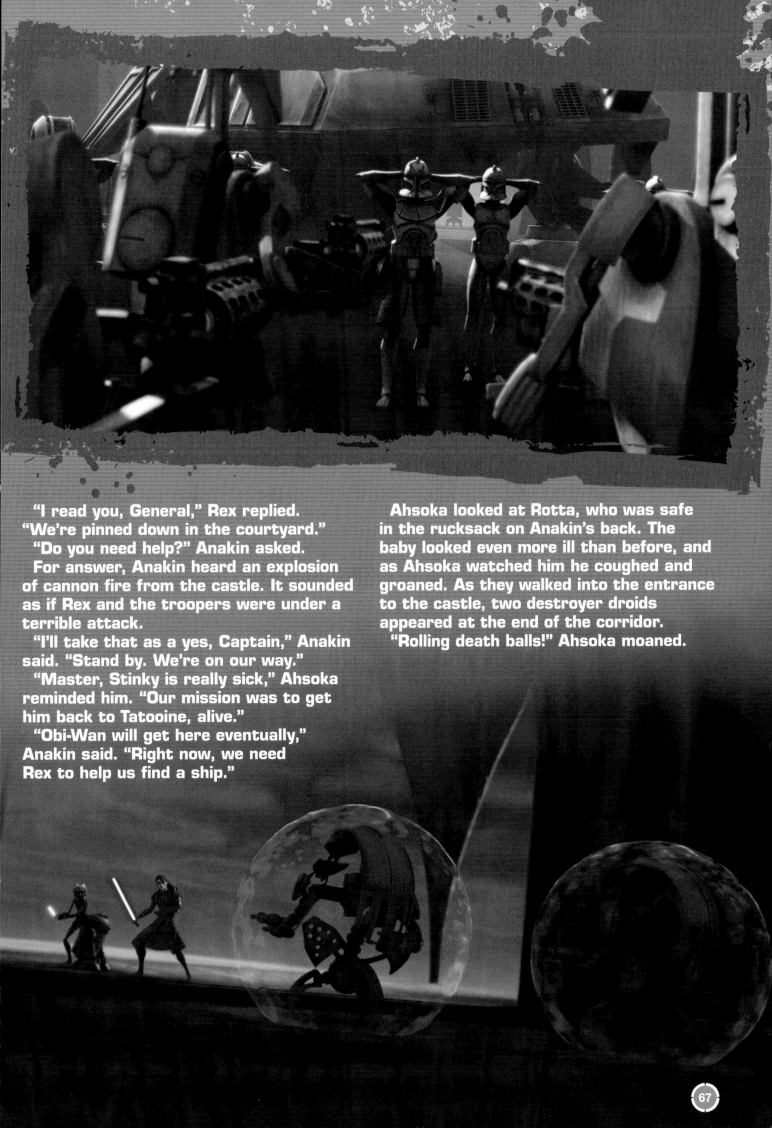

"I read you, General," Rex replied. "We're pinned down in the courtyard."

"Do you need help?" Anakin asked.

For answer, Anakin heard an explosion of cannon fire from the castle. It sounded as if Rex and the troopers were under a terrible attack.

"I'll take that as a yes, Captain," Anakin said. "Stand by. We're on our way."

"Master, Stinky is really sick," Ahsoka reminded him. "Our mission was to get him back to Tatooine, alive."

"Obi-Wan will get here eventually," Anakin said. "Right now, we need Rex to help us find a ship."

Ahsoka looked at Rotta, who was safe in the rucksack on Anakin's back. The baby looked even more ill than before, and as Ahsoka watched him he coughed and groaned. As they walked into the entrance to the castle, two destroyer droids appeared at the end of the corridor.

"Rolling death balls!" Ahsoka moaned.

Anakin and Ahsoka switched on their lightsabers and defended themselves against the droids' laser fire. They backed out on to the landing platform, but the rolling droids kept moving towards them. Ventress was behind them with her lightsabers at the ready.

"Artoo, the door!" Anakin cried.

R2 closed the door just in time, but they were not going to be safe for long. Ventress started to cut a hole through the door with her lightsabers.

The landing platform shuddered under their feet as spider droids attacked it far below. The situation looked dire, but then Rotta began to point and squeal.

"Not now, Stinky!" Aksoka cried.

But the little Hutt had seen something sparkling in the distance. On top of another rock, there was a landing platform . . . and on that landing platform was a ship!

"Master, look!" Ahsoka cried.

"Just what we need!" Anakin exclaimed.

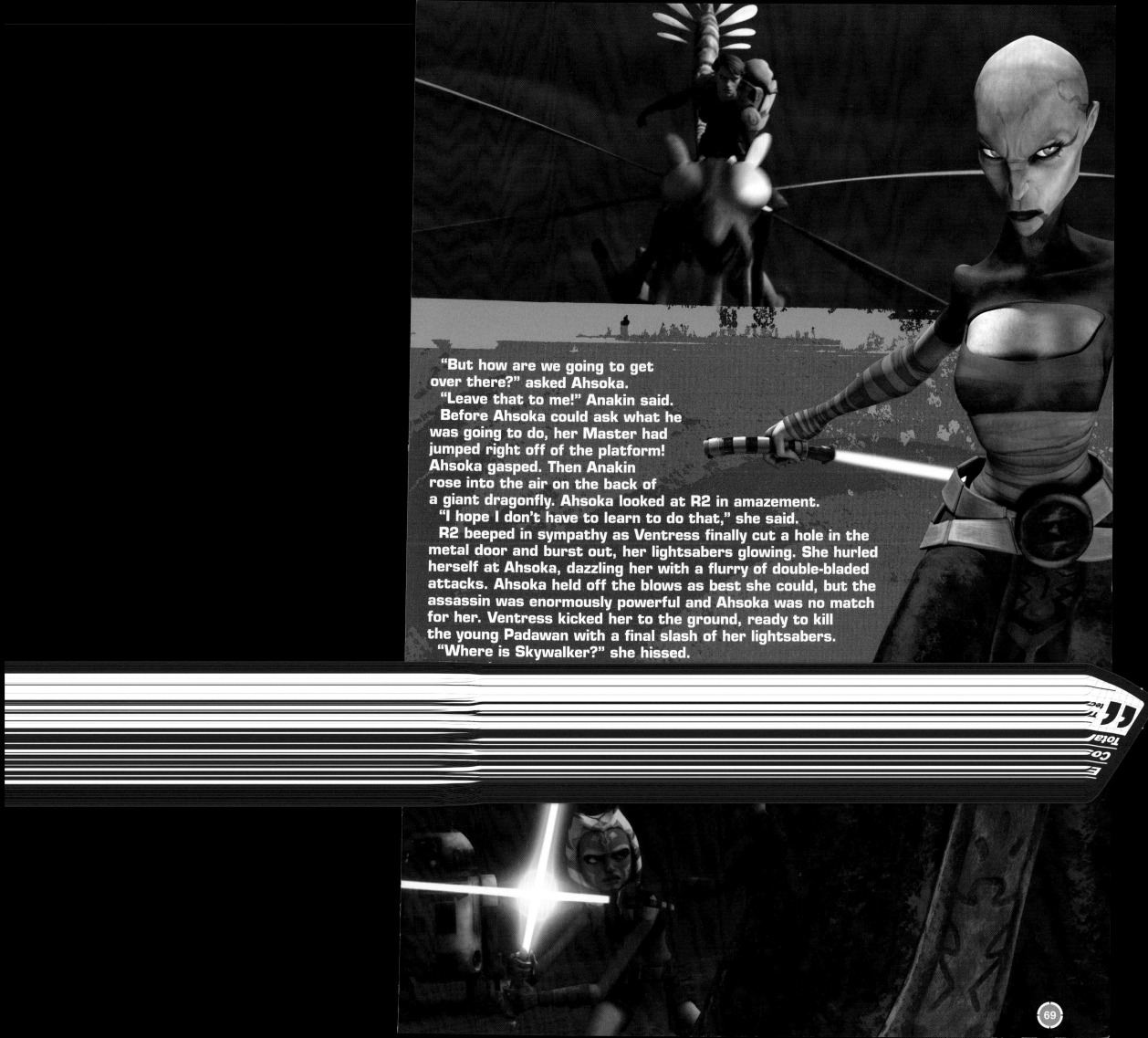

"But how are we going to get over there?" asked Ahsoka.

"Leave that to me!" Anakin said.

Before Ahsoka could ask what he was going to do, her Master had jumped right off of the platform! Ahsoka gasped. Then Anakin rose into the air on the back of a giant dragonfly. Ahsoka looked at R2 in amazement.

"I hope I don't have to learn to do that," she said.

R2 beeped in sympathy as Ventress finally cut a hole in the metal door and burst out, her lightsabers glowing. She hurled herself at Ahsoka, dazzling her with a flurry of double-bladed attacks. Ahsoka held off the blows as best she could, but the assassin was enormously powerful and Ahsoka was no match for her. Ventress kicked her to the ground, ready to kill the young Padawan with a final slash of her lightsabers.

"Where is Skywalker?" she hissed.

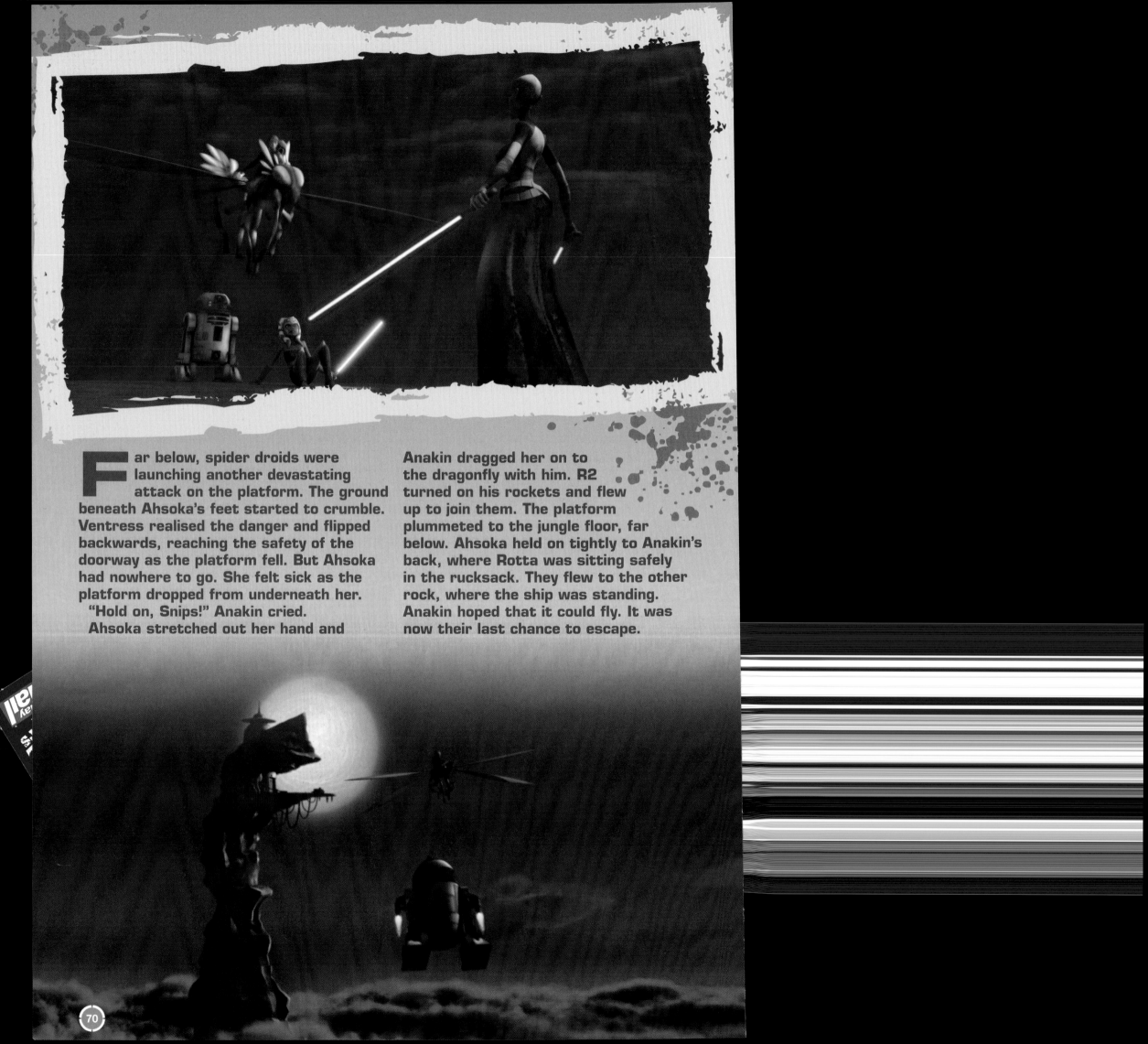

Far below, spider droids were launching another devastating attack on the platform. The ground beneath Ahsoka's feet started to crumble. Ventress realised the danger and flipped backwards, reaching the safety of the doorway as the platform fell. But Ahsoka had nowhere to go. She felt sick as the platform dropped from underneath her.

"Hold on, Snips!" Anakin cried.

Ahsoka stretched out her hand and Anakin dragged her on to the dragonfly with him. R2 turned on his rockets and flew up to join them. The platform plummeted to the jungle floor, far below. Ahsoka held on tightly to Anakin's back, where Rotta was sitting safely in the rucksack. They flew to the other rock, where the ship was standing. Anakin hoped that it could fly. It was now their last chance to escape.

High above the planet surface, vulture droid fighters were attacking Obi-Wan Kenobi and his fleet. Obi-Wan was in the middle of the action, zooming around the fighters and blasting them out of the sky. At last he and his men destroyed most of the vulture droids. He could see smoke rising up from the castle and guessed that there was trouble down there.

"It looks like there's some kind of battle on the east side of the palace," Obi-Wan told his men. "And if there's a battle, Anakin's probably in the middle of it. We'll start looking for him there."

Meanwhile, Anakin and Ahsoka had arrived on the landing pad with R2. Their hearts sank. The ship that had looked so shiny and perfect from the distance was nothing more than an old, scruffy rust-bucket of a freighter. On the side of the ship the name *Twilight* was written in faded paint.

71

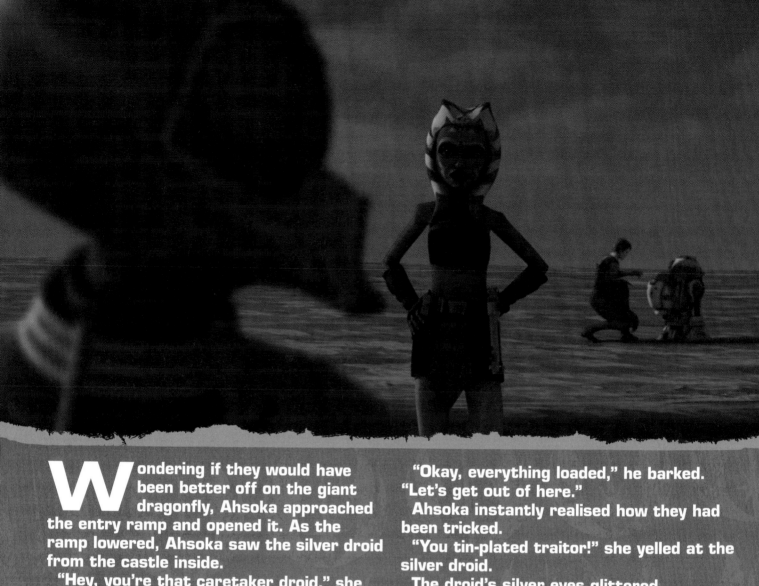

Wondering if they would have been better off on the giant dragonfly, Ahsoka approached the entry ramp and opened it. As the ramp lowered, Ahsoka saw the silver droid from the castle inside.

"Hey, you're that caretaker droid," she said. "I wondered what happened to you."

The droid seemed surprised to see her.

"Okay, everything loaded," he barked. "Let's get out of here."

Ahsoka instantly realised how they had been tricked.

"You tin-plated traitor!" she yelled at the silver droid.

The droid's silver eyes glittered.

"Blast her!" he ordered.

Several battle droids surged towards

In the castle courtyard, Obi-Wan came to the rescue of Rex and his troops, and then hurried into the castle, thinking Anakin was inside. In the entry corridor he found a squad of super battle droids surrounding Ventress. She activated her lightsabers.

"Master Kenobi," she sneered. "Always chasing after Skywalker. How predictable."

"Anakin leaves quite a mess," Obi-Wan replied. "Which always leads me to you, Ventress."

"Take him!" Ventress told her droids.

She ran through a door at the side of the corridor. Obi-Wan quickly destroyed the droids and chased after Ventress. She had entered a dark room that was full of tall columns. Obi-Wan moved slowly, using the Force to guide him.

"Ventress, I know you're here," he said. "You can't hide. I feel your frustration. Let me guess: You're after Jabba's son, too."

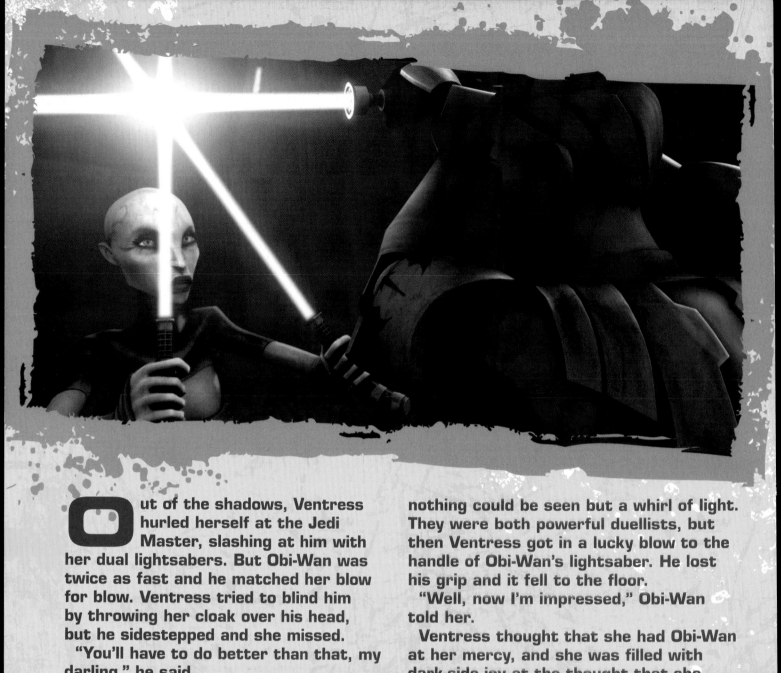

Out of the shadows, Ventress hurled herself at the Jedi Master, slashing at him with her dual lightsabers. But Obi-Wan was twice as fast and he matched her blow for blow. Ventress tried to blind him by throwing her cloak over his head, but he sidestepped and she missed.

"You'll have to do better than that, my darling," he said.

Ventress was as enraged as Obi-Wan was calm. Their battle was so fast that nothing could be seen but a whirl of light. They were both powerful duellists, but then Ventress got in a lucky blow to the handle of Obi-Wan's lightsaber. He lost his grip and it fell to the floor.

"Well, now I'm impressed," Obi-Wan told her.

Ventress thought that she had Obi-Wan at her mercy, and she was filled with dark-side joy at the thought that she would destroy him.

"Now you die!" she screeched.

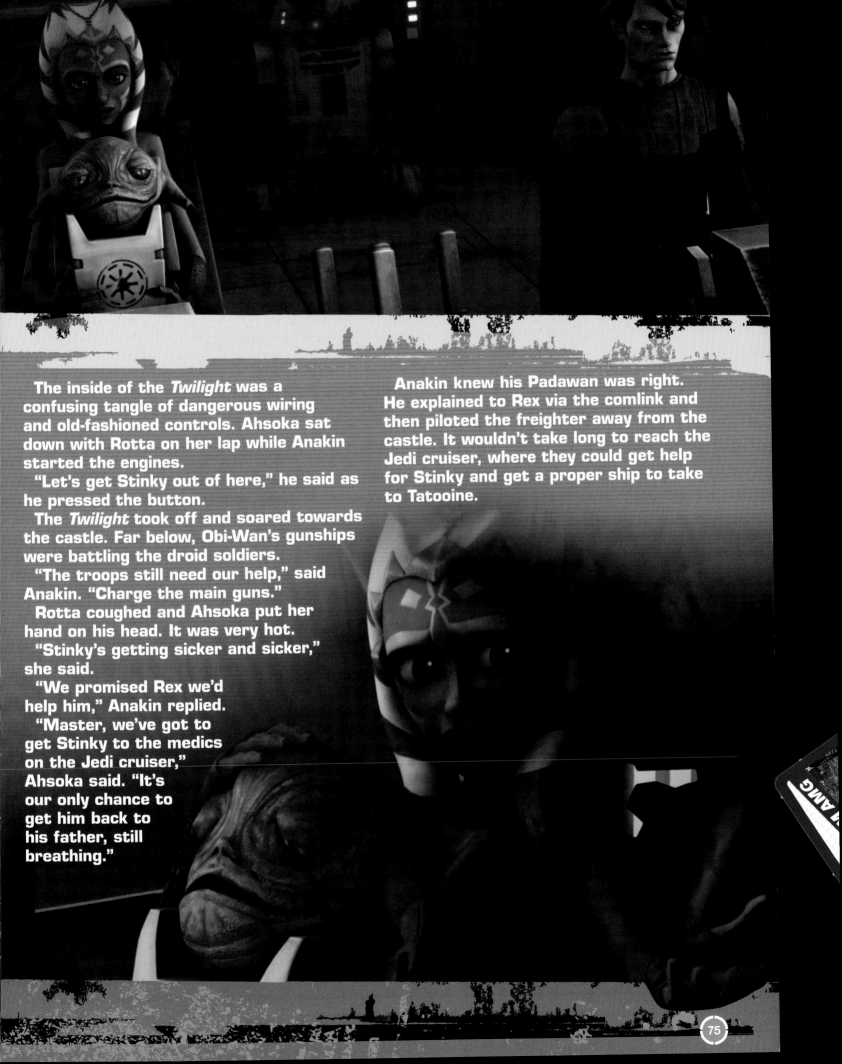

The inside of the *Twilight* was a confusing tangle of dangerous wiring and old-fashioned controls. Ahsoka sat down with Rotta on her lap while Anakin started the engines.

"Let's get Stinky out of here," he said as he pressed the button.

The *Twilight* took off and soared towards the castle. Far below, Obi-Wan's gunships were battling the droid soldiers.

"The troops still need our help," said Anakin. "Charge the main guns."

Rotta coughed and Ahsoka put her hand on his head. It was very hot.

"Stinky's getting sicker and sicker," she said.

"We promised Rex we'd help him," Anakin replied.

"Master, we've got to get Stinky to the medics on the Jedi cruiser," Ahsoka said. "It's our only chance to get him back to his father, still breathing."

Anakin knew his Padawan was right. He explained to Rex via the comlink and then piloted the freighter away from the castle. It wouldn't take long to reach the Jedi cruiser, where they could get help for Stinky and get a proper ship to take to Tatooine.

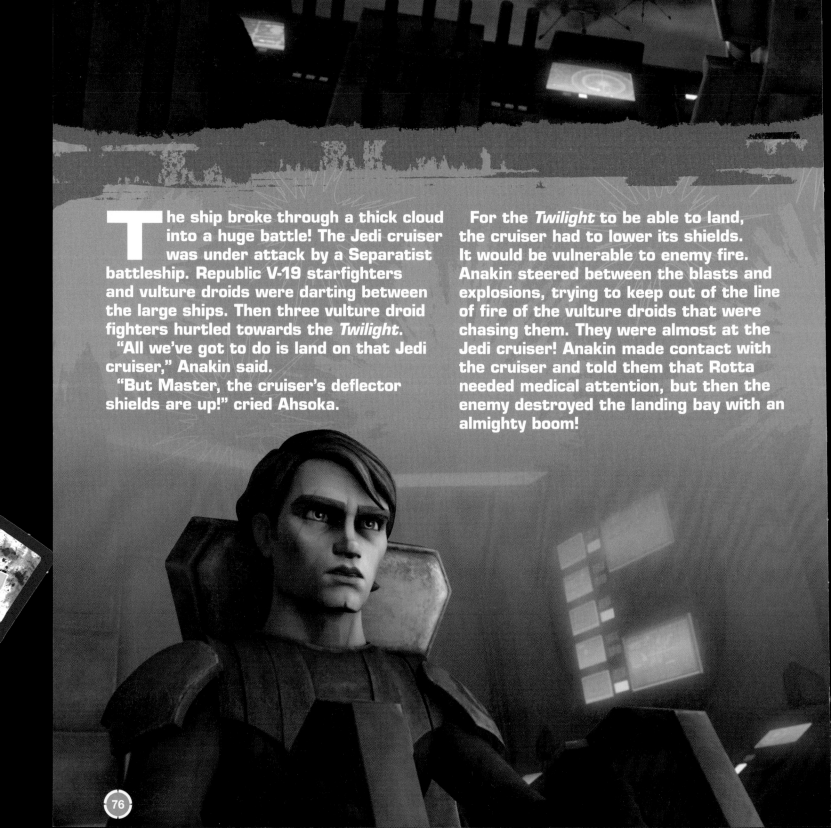

The ship broke through a thick cloud into a huge battle! The Jedi cruiser was under attack by a Separatist battleship. Republic V-19 starfighters and vulture droids were darting between the large ships. Then three vulture droid fighters hurtled towards the *Twilight*.

"All we've got to do is land on that Jedi cruiser," Anakin said.

"But Master, the cruiser's deflector shields are up!" cried Ahsoka.

For the *Twilight* to be able to land, the cruiser had to lower its shields. It would be vulnerable to enemy fire. Anakin steered between the blasts and explosions, trying to keep out of the line of fire of the vulture droids that were chasing them. They were almost at the Jedi cruiser! Anakin made contact with the cruiser and told them that Rotta needed medical attention, but then the enemy destroyed the landing bay with an almighty boom!

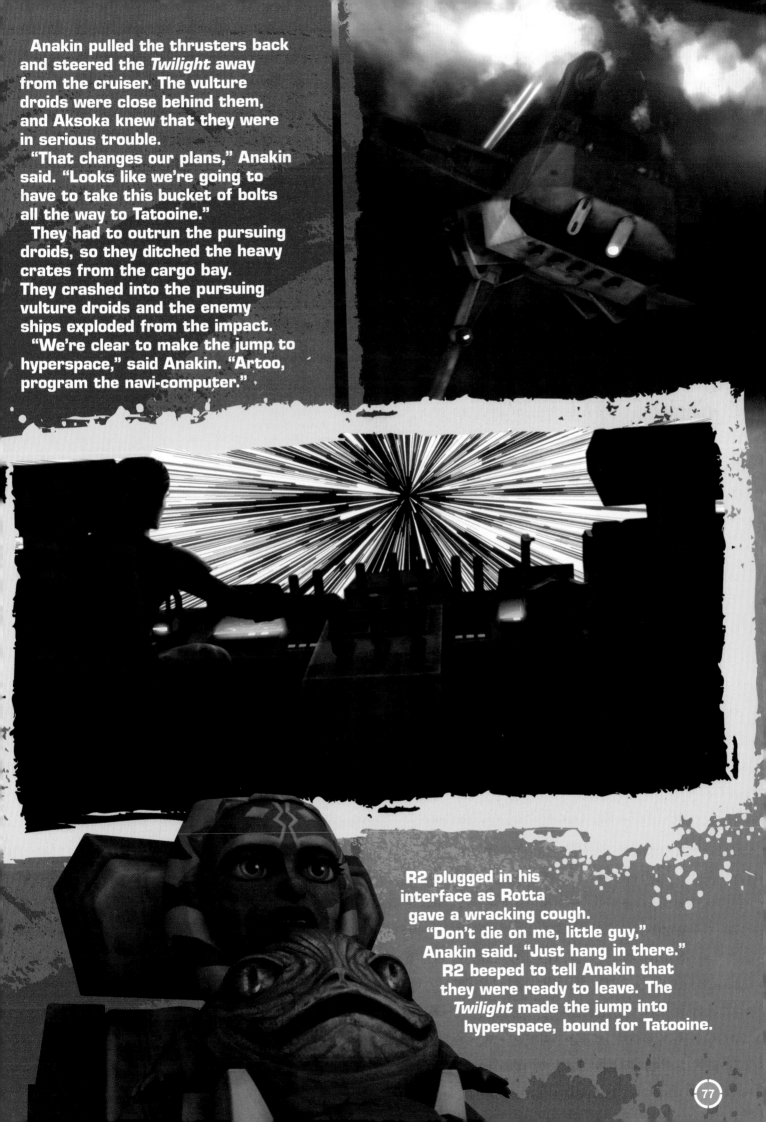

Anakin pulled the thrusters back and steered the *Twilight* away from the cruiser. The vulture droids were close behind them, and Aksoka knew that they were in serious trouble.

"That changes our plans," Anakin said. "Looks like we're going to have to take this bucket of bolts all the way to Tatooine."

They had to outrun the pursuing droids, so they ditched the heavy crates from the cargo bay. They crashed into the pursuing vulture droids and the enemy ships exploded from the impact.

"We're clear to make the jump to hyperspace," said Anakin. "Artoo, program the navi-computer."

R2 plugged in his interface as Rotta gave a wracking cough.
"Don't die on me, little guy," Anakin said. "Just hang in there."
R2 beeped to tell Anakin that they were ready to leave. The *Twilight* made the jump into hyperspace, bound for Tatooine.

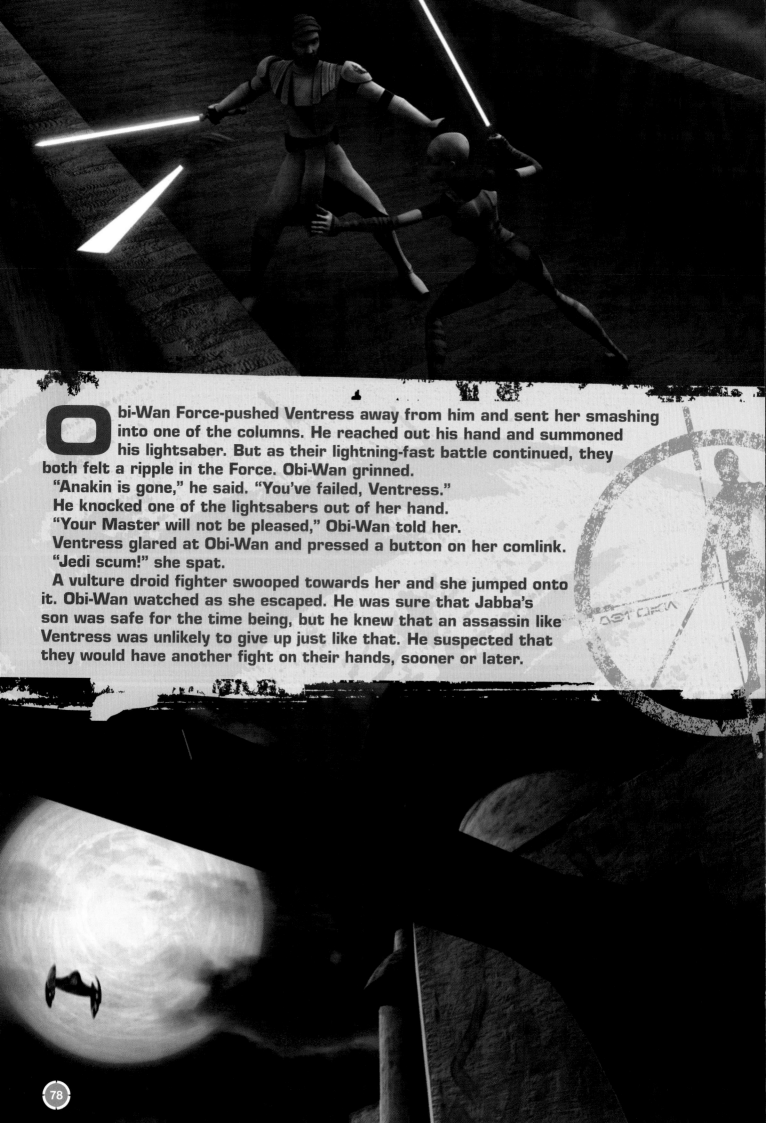

Obi-Wan Force-pushed Ventress away from him and sent her smashing into one of the columns. He reached out his hand and summoned his lightsaber. But as their lightning-fast battle continued, they both felt a ripple in the Force. Obi-Wan grinned.

"Anakin is gone," he said. "You've failed, Ventress."

He knocked one of the lightsabers out of her hand.

"Your Master will not be pleased," Obi-Wan told her.

Ventress glared at Obi-Wan and pressed a button on her comlink. "Jedi scum!" she spat.

A vulture droid fighter swooped towards her and she jumped onto it. Obi-Wan watched as she escaped. He was sure that Jabba's son was safe for the time being, but he knew that an assassin like Ventress was unlikely to give up just like that. He suspected that they would have another fight on their hands, sooner or later.

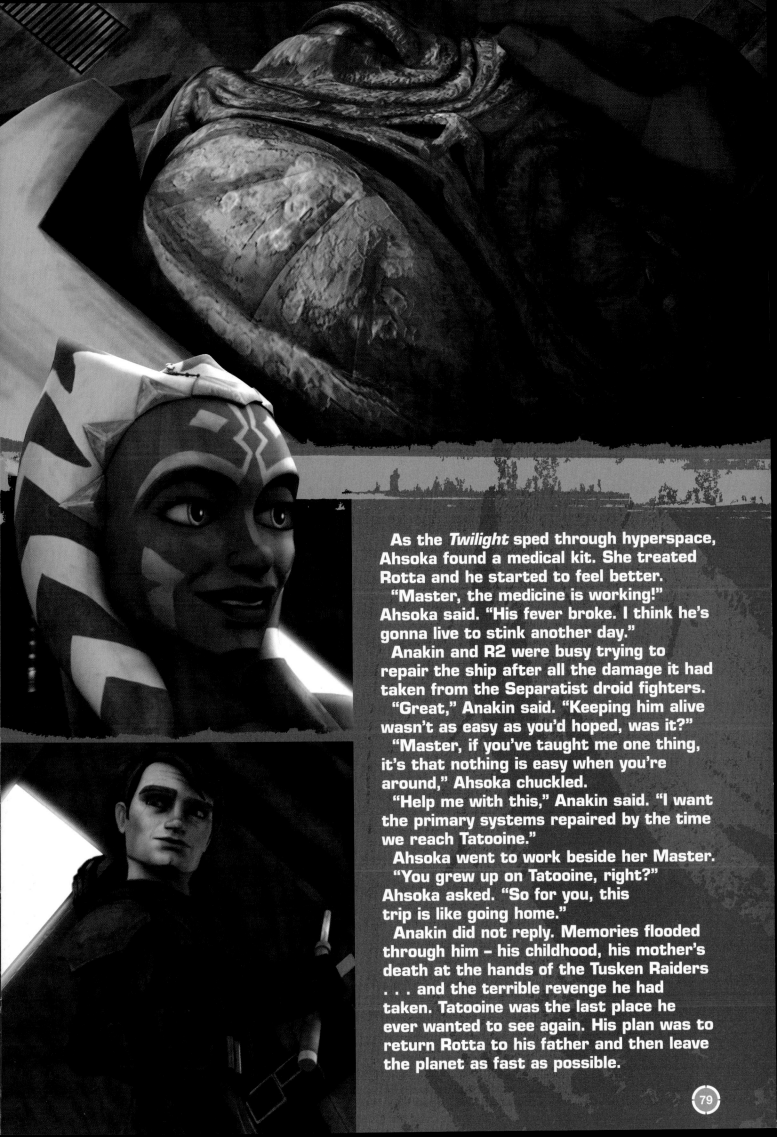

As the *Twilight* sped through hyperspace, Ahsoka found a medical kit. She treated Rotta and he started to feel better.

"Master, the medicine is working!" Ahsoka said. "His fever broke. I think he's gonna live to stink another day."

Anakin and R2 were busy trying to repair the ship after all the damage it had taken from the Separatist droid fighters.

"Great," Anakin said. "Keeping him alive wasn't as easy as you'd hoped, was it?"

"Master, if you've taught me one thing, it's that nothing is easy when you're around," Ahsoka chuckled.

"Help me with this," Anakin said. "I want the primary systems repaired by the time we reach Tatooine."

Ahsoka went to work beside her Master.

"You grew up on Tatooine, right?" Ahsoka asked. "So for you, this trip is like going home."

Anakin did not reply. Memories flooded through him – his childhood, his mother's death at the hands of the Tusken Raiders . . . and the terrible revenge he had taken. Tatooine was the last place he ever wanted to see again. His plan was to return Rotta to his father and then leave the planet as fast as possible.

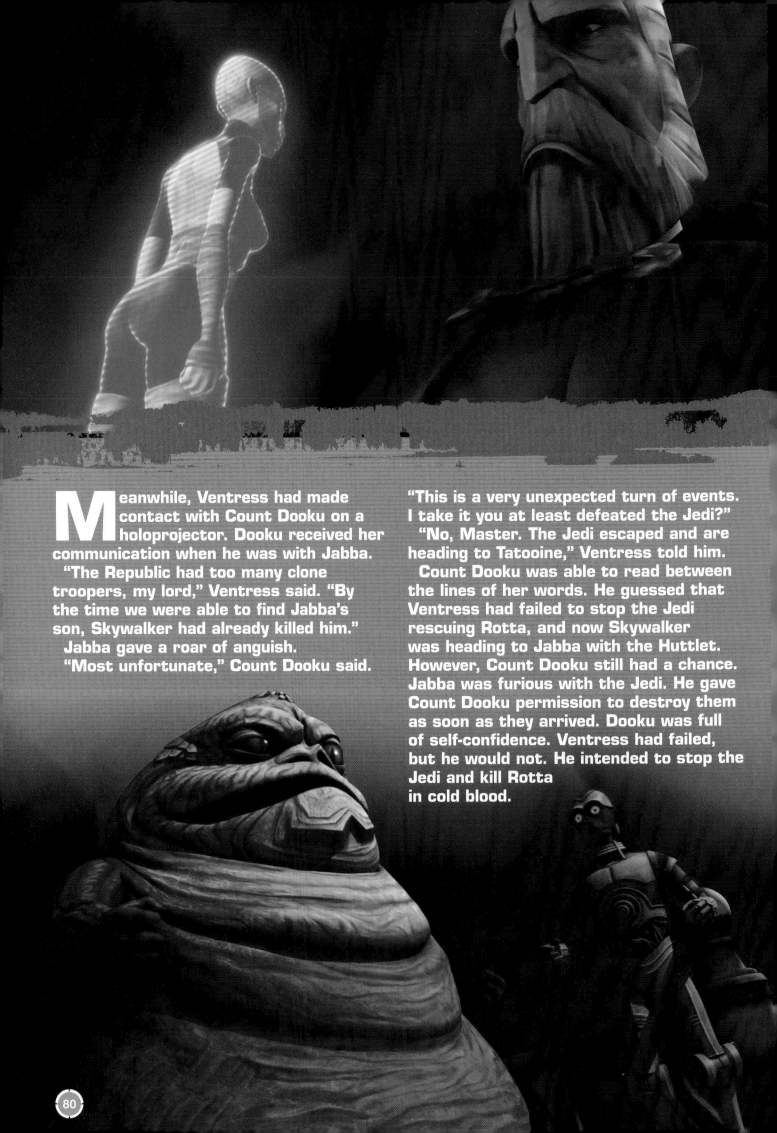

Meanwhile, Ventress had made contact with Count Dooku on a holoprojector. Dooku received her communication when he was with Jabba.

"The Republic had too many clone troopers, my lord," Ventress said. "By the time we were able to find Jabba's son, Skywalker had already killed him."

Jabba gave a roar of anguish.

"Most unfortunate," Count Dooku said.

"This is a very unexpected turn of events. I take it you at least defeated the Jedi?"

"No, Master. The Jedi escaped and are heading to Tatooine," Ventress told him.

Count Dooku was able to read between the lines of her words. He guessed that Ventress had failed to stop the Jedi rescuing Rotta, and now Skywalker was heading to Jabba with the Huttlet. However, Count Dooku still had a chance. Jabba was furious with the Jedi. He gave Count Dooku permission to destroy them as soon as they arrived. Dooku was full of self-confidence. Ventress had failed, but he would not. He intended to stop the Jedi and kill Rotta in cold blood.

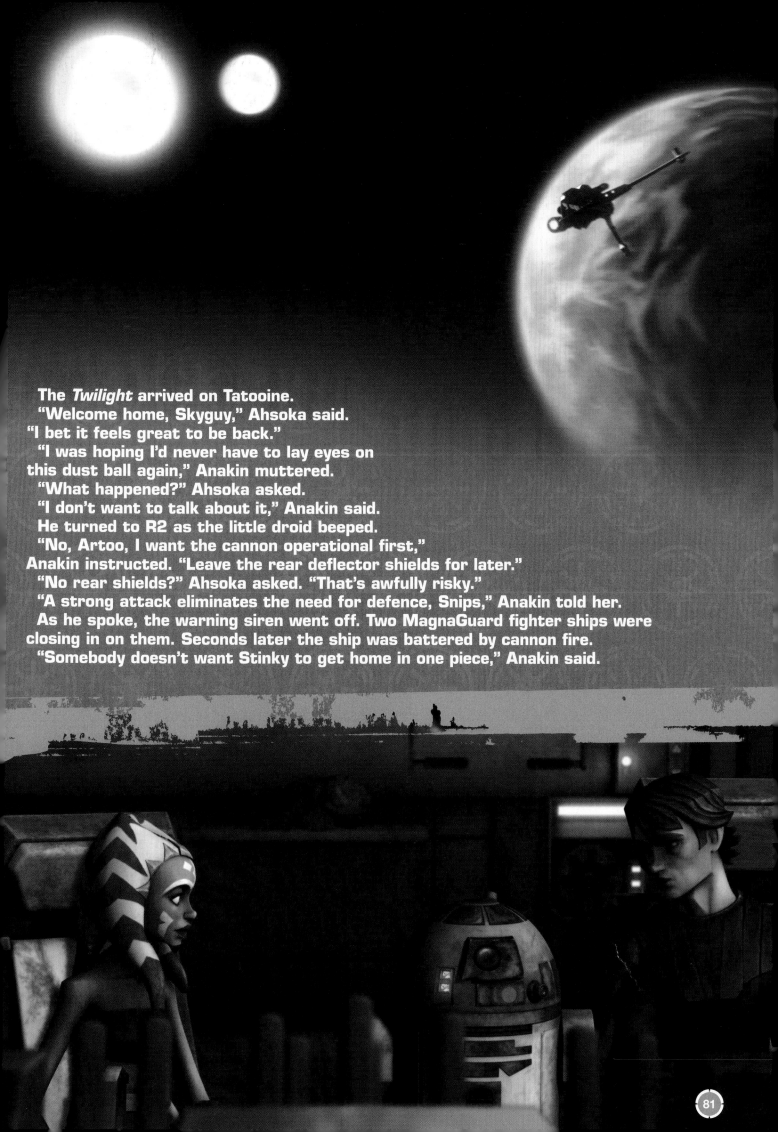

The *Twilight* arrived on Tatooine.

"Welcome home, Skyguy," Ahsoka said. "I bet it feels great to be back."

"I was hoping I'd never have to lay eyes on this dust ball again," Anakin muttered.

"What happened?" Ahsoka asked.

"I don't want to talk about it," Anakin said. He turned to R2 as the little droid beeped.

"No, Artoo, I want the cannon operational first," Anakin instructed. "Leave the rear deflector shields for later."

"No rear shields?" Ahsoka asked. "That's awfully risky."

"A strong attack eliminates the need for defence, Snips," Anakin told her.

As he spoke, the warning siren went off. Two MagnaGuard fighter ships were closing in on them. Seconds later the ship was battered by cannon fire.

"Somebody doesn't want Stinky to get home in one piece," Anakin said.

The cockpit shook under another assault from the fighters.
"Ahsoka, activate the guns!" Anakin cried.
Ahsoka reached for the controls and a series of lights flashed in front of her.
"All the guns are locked in the forward position," she reported. "It's too bad you decided not to repair the rear deflector shields."

"Not now, Ahsoka!" Anakin said, trying to finish repairing the engineering panel. "Artoo, see if you can unlock those guns!"

"'Sometimes a good defence is the best offence'," Ahsoka muttered.

Anakin gave her a stern look. Then the ship was hit by another blast of furious fire. Anakin took his place in the pilot's chair and released a cannon blast, exploding one of the MagnaGuard fighters. The second fighter circled around them, trying to attack from behind. With a sinking feeling, Anakin saw a piece of their rear hull exploding into pieces. The *Twilight* groaned and creaked like something dying.

"I think we needed those rear shields after all," he admitted. "Artoo! Turn those guns around!"

R2 fired, but the MagnaGuard fighter managed to zip out of the way. It wheeled around and returned fire, blasting the rear of the *Twilight* again. R2 took aim for a second attempt. This time he got a direct hit and the MagnaGuard fighter burst into flames. However, there was no time to celebrate. They had destroyed their enemies, but the *Twilight* still had to land, and it was badly damaged.

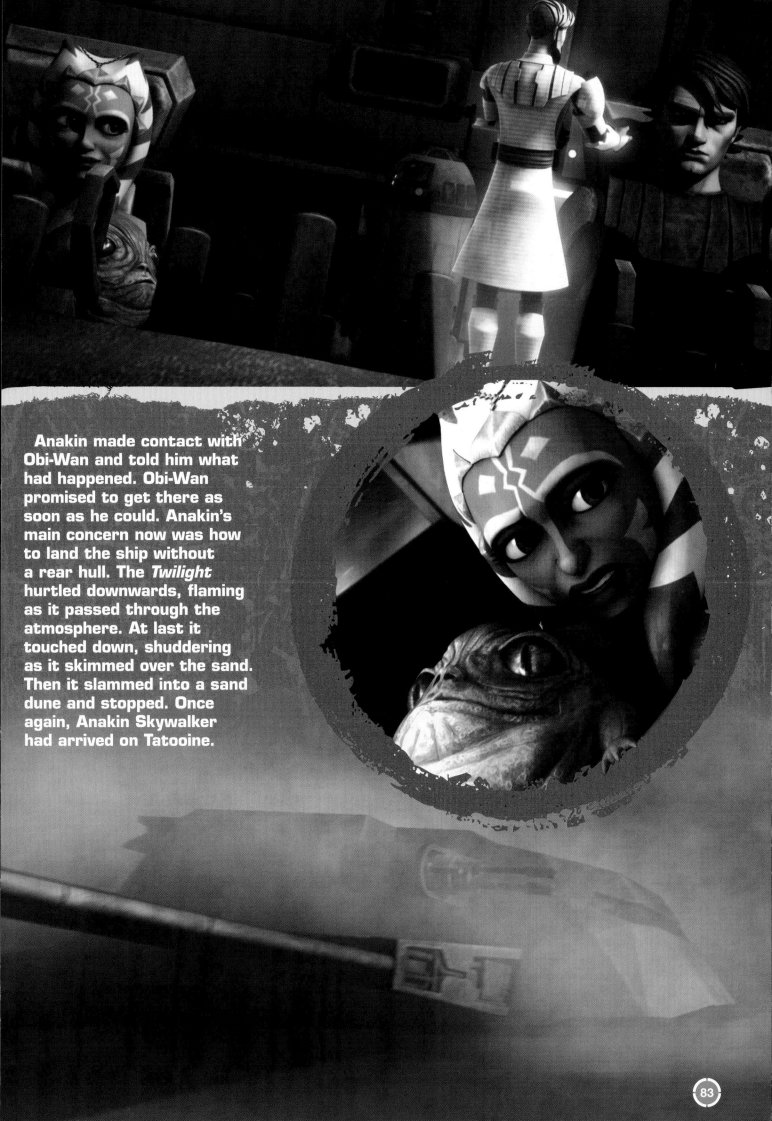

Anakin made contact with Obi-Wan and told him what had happened. Obi-Wan promised to get there as soon as he could. Anakin's main concern now was how to land the ship without a rear hull. The *Twilight* hurtled downwards, flaming as it passed through the atmosphere. At last it touched down, shuddering as it skimmed over the sand. Then it slammed into a sand dune and stopped. Once again, Anakin Skywalker had arrived on Tatooine.

JEDI DOOR HANGER

Sometimes you need privacy to focus on your connection with the Living Force. This door hanger will tell your family whether they can disturb you or not!

COME IN

and May the Force Be With You!

1) Trace or copy the design opposite onto a piece of white card.

2) Trim the card to the right shape.

3) Trace the other side of the hanger on to the other side of the card.

4) Colour it in! Make sure you get all the colours right.

5) Place the hanger over your bedroom doorknob to show whether you want visitors or not.

KEEP OUT

Jedi in Training!

You can use this design to make cool door hangers for all your friends and family!

The Jedi have intercepted some secret messages, but they're in code. Crack the code to find the hidden messages. Fill in the code breaker below as you figure out what each letter stands for. (Some have already been filled in to help you out.) Then make up your own secret messages!

1) ZAZSRA CSEUZJSGL YZC Z AGU BZPZUZA. →

2) PZLVY CRPRKMC RC OKAVLKJJRAH VYG OJKAG UZLC. →

3) VYG CRVY URJJ LRCG ZHZRA. →

4) ZCZII DGAVLGCC BJZAC VK PMGJ KFR-UZA SGAKFR. →

5) VYG OYKCGA KAG URJJ FLRAH FZJZAOG VK VYG QKLOG. →

A	B	C	D	E	F	G	H	I	J	K	L	M
N						E	G			L		R

N	O	P	Q	R	S	T	U	V	W	X	Y	Z
C		F		K							N	A

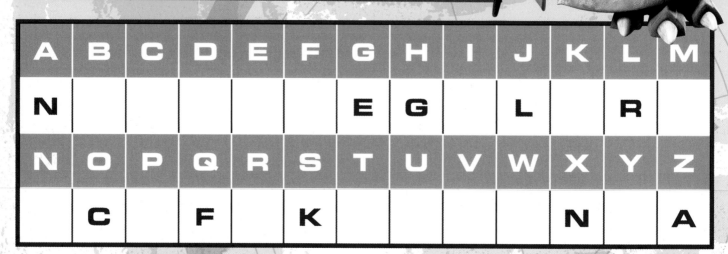

CLONE WARS CROSSWORD

Solve the clues and fill in the answers to discover the name of a galactic weapon.

1.
2.
3.
4.
5.
6.
7.

1) Who was Anakin's Master when he was a Padawan?

2) What relation is Ziro to Jabba?

3) What is the name of Jabba the Hutt's son?

4) What is Anakin's pet name for his Padawan?

5) What is Ahsoka's surname?

6) Which clone captain is second in command to Anakin Skywalker?

7) On which planet did Anakin meet Ahsoka for the first time?

GALACTIC WEAPON =

High Flyers

1 **2** **3**

A. COUNT DOOKU   B. OBI-WAN KENOBI   C. ANAKIN SKYWALKER

Who flies what? Can you connect the characters to their crafts?

1	2	3	4	5	6

D. PADMÉ AMIDALA

E. CLONE TROOPER

F. JABBA THE HUTT

Far away on planet Coruscant, Yoda had a meeting with Chancellor Palpatine. Together they watched a hologram of Obi-Wan as he reported on recent events.

"Anakin reached Tatooine with the Huttlet, Master," Obi-Wan said. "But he's still in grave danger. Separatist troops are desperate to intercept him. I think this whole plot was engineered by Dooku to convince Jabba we kidnapped his son."

"If believe this the Hutts do, ended our chance of a treaty with them will be," murmured Yoda. "Join Dooku and the Separatists, Jabba will. Yes."

"That would be a disaster," Chancellor Palpatine said. "We *must* have this allegiance with the Hutts if we are to win the war in the Outer Rim."

"In Skywalker is the Republic's only hope," said Yoda. "Return Jabba's son, he must."

As Obi-Wan's image disappeared, Senator Padmé Amidala arrived in the Chancellor's office. Palpatine and Yoda smiled and greeted her.

"Master Yoda, so good to see you," said Padmé.

"Good it is to see you, Senator," Yoda replied.

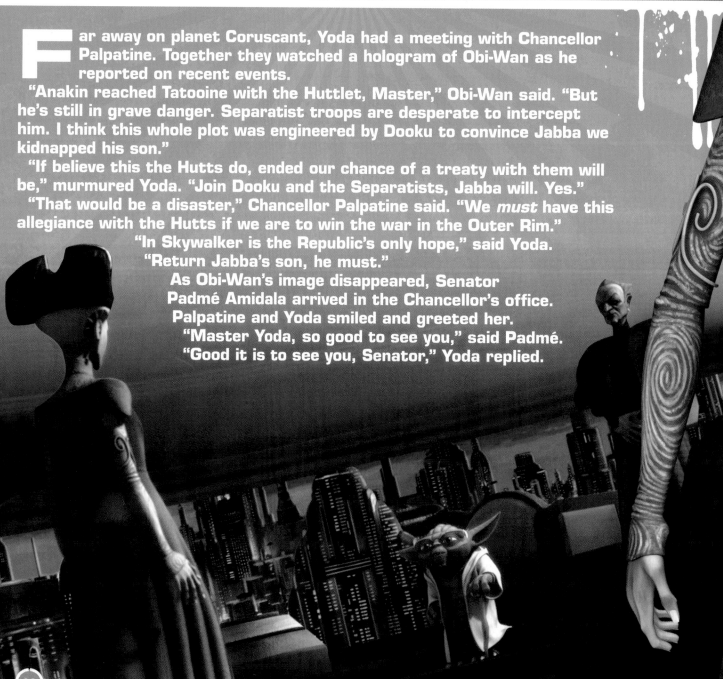

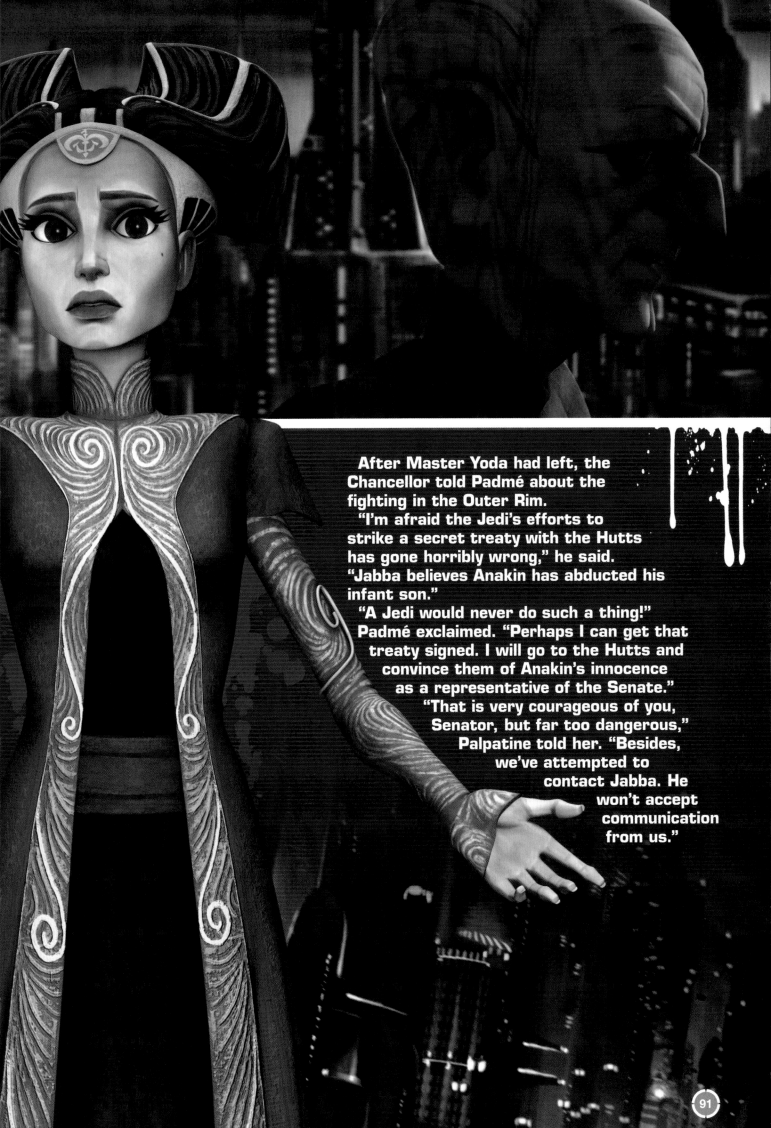

After Master Yoda had left, the Chancellor told Padmé about the fighting in the Outer Rim.

"I'm afraid the Jedi's efforts to strike a secret treaty with the Hutts has gone horribly wrong," he said. "Jabba believes Anakin has abducted his infant son."

"A Jedi would never do such a thing!" Padmé exclaimed. "Perhaps I can get that treaty signed. I will go to the Hutts and convince them of Anakin's innocence as a representative of the Senate."

"That is very courageous of you, Senator, but far too dangerous," Palpatine told her. "Besides, we've attempted to contact Jabba. He won't accept communication from us."

"Jabba the Hutt has an uncle in the old downtown area here in Coruscant," Padmé remembered. "Perhaps I can reason with him and reopen negotiations."

"Please, my dear, I beg you, reconsider this," said Palpatine, looking worried.

"Don't worry, Chancellor," Padmé replied.

"I've dealt with far worse than the Hutts."

Padmé lived in fear and heartache every time her secret husband went off into the galaxy to fight a battle, and now her fears seemed to be coming true. Anakin's life might be in danger; she couldn't stand by and do nothing. She took a transport to the Hutt palace that towered over the streets of downtown Coruscant.

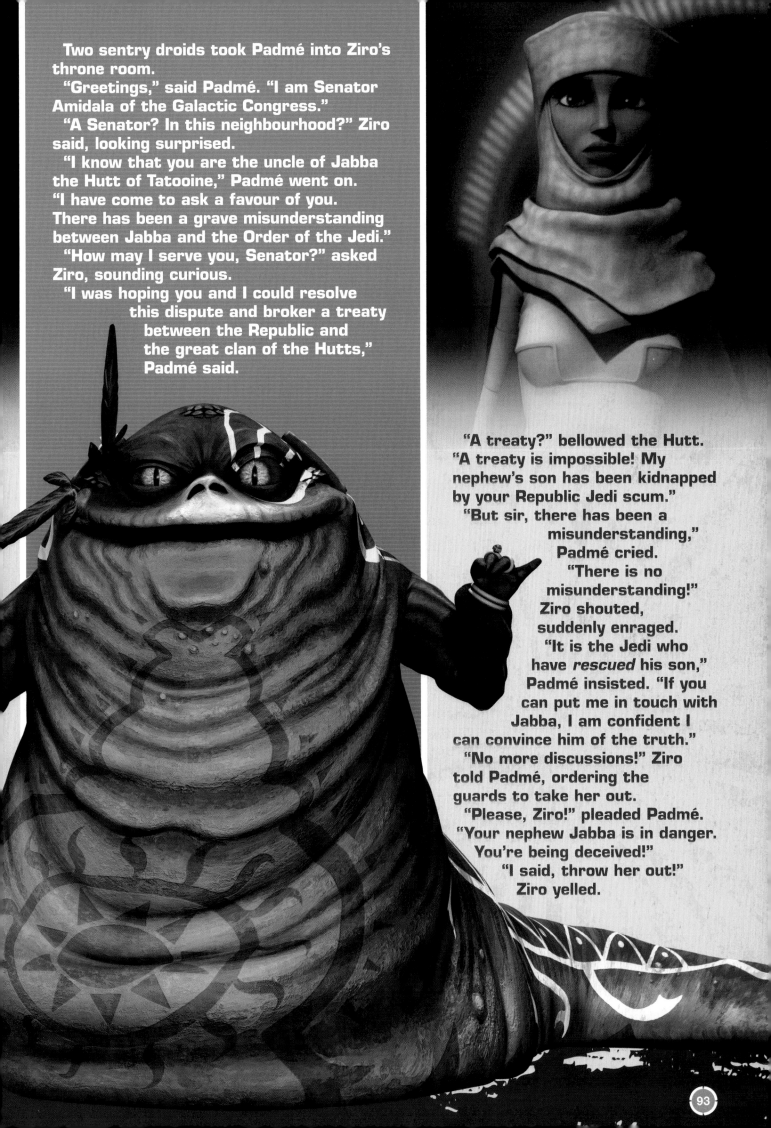

Two sentry droids took Padmé into Ziro's throne room.

"Greetings," said Padmé. "I am Senator Amidala of the Galactic Congress."

"A Senator? In this neighbourhood?" Ziro said, looking surprised.

"I know that you are the uncle of Jabba the Hutt of Tatooine," Padmé went on. "I have come to ask a favour of you. There has been a grave misunderstanding between Jabba and the Order of the Jedi."

"How may I serve you, Senator?" asked Ziro, sounding curious.

"I was hoping you and I could resolve this dispute and broker a treaty between the Republic and the great clan of the Hutts," Padmé said.

"A treaty?" bellowed the Hutt. "A treaty is impossible! My nephew's son has been kidnapped by your Republic Jedi scum."

"But sir, there has been a misunderstanding," Padmé cried.

"There is no misunderstanding!" Ziro shouted, suddenly enraged.

"It is the Jedi who have *rescued* his son," Padmé insisted. "If you can put me in touch with Jabba, I am confident I can convince him of the truth."

"No more discussions!" Ziro told Padmé, ordering the guards to take her out.

"Please, Ziro!" pleaded Padmé. "Your nephew Jabba is in danger. You're being deceived!"

"I said, throw her out!" Ziro yelled.

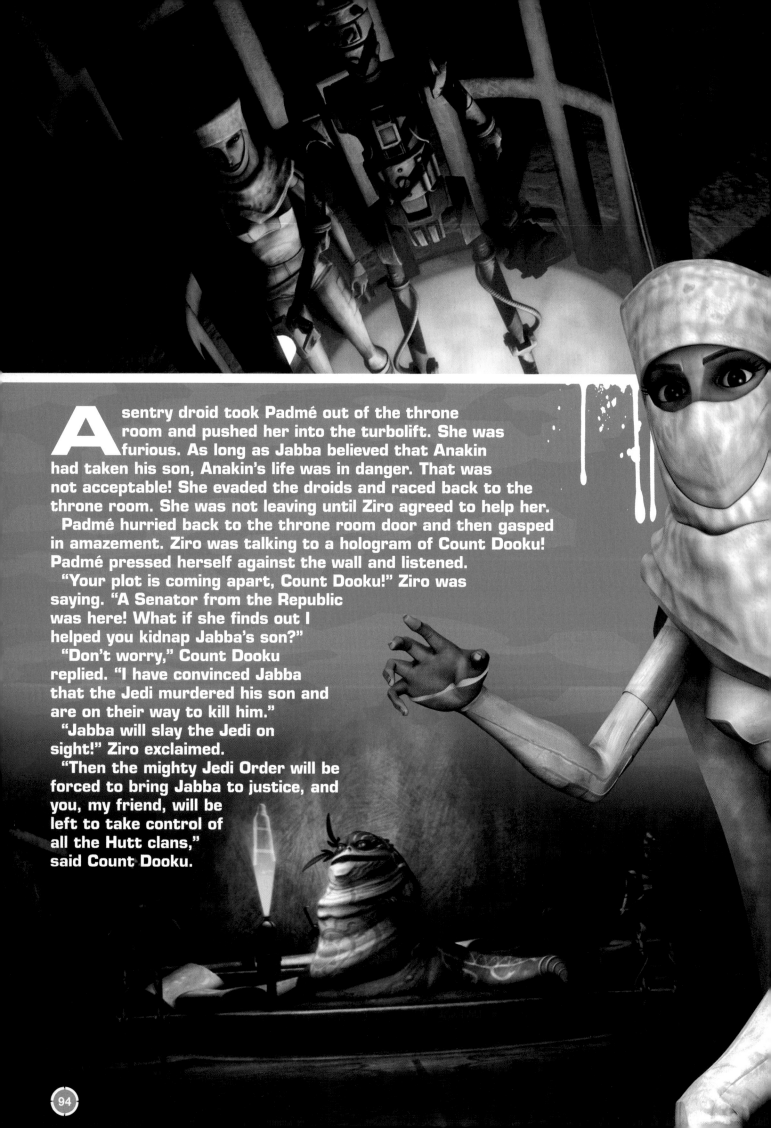

A sentry droid took Padmé out of the throne room and pushed her into the turbolift. She was furious. As long as Jabba believed that Anakin had taken his son, Anakin's life was in danger. That was not acceptable! She evaded the droids and raced back to the throne room. She was not leaving until Ziro agreed to help her.

Padmé hurried back to the throne room door and then gasped in amazement. Ziro was talking to a hologram of Count Dooku! Padmé pressed herself against the wall and listened.

"Your plot is coming apart, Count Dooku!" Ziro was saying. "A Senator from the Republic was here! What if she finds out I helped you kidnap Jabba's son?"

"Don't worry," Count Dooku replied. "I have convinced Jabba that the Jedi murdered his son and are on their way to kill him."

"Jabba will slay the Jedi on sight!" Ziro exclaimed.

"Then the mighty Jedi Order will be forced to bring Jabba to justice, and you, my friend, will be left to take control of all the Hutt clans," said Count Dooku.

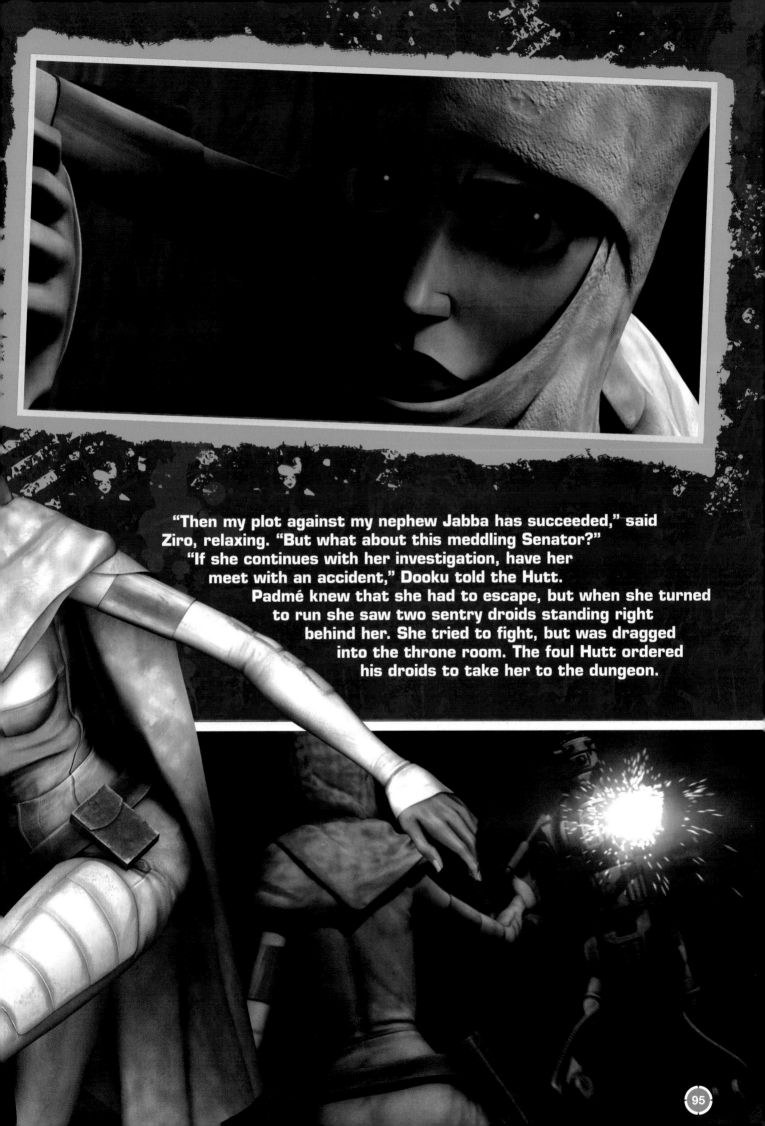

"Then my plot against my nephew Jabba has succeeded," said Ziro, relaxing. "But what about this meddling Senator?"
"If she continues with her investigation, have her meet with an accident," Dooku told the Hutt.
Padmé knew that she had to escape, but when she turned to run she saw two sentry droids standing right behind her. She tried to fight, but was dragged into the throne room. The foul Hutt ordered his droids to take her to the dungeon.

On Tatooine, Ahsoka stepped out of the *Twilight* on to the sand. She was holding Rotta in her arms and she gazed around with curiosity.

"Welcome home, Stinky," she said.

Anakin was right behind them. He took the rucksack that Rotta sat in and put it on.

"Jabba's palace is on the far side of the Dune Sea," he said. "We'd better hurry if we're going to make it by morning."

R2 beeped and sped down the ramp after them.

Both Tatooine's suns began to sink as Anakin, Ahsoka and R2 made their way slowly towards the Hutt palace. It was going to take a long time to get there, but Anakin was not in a talkative mood. Ahsoka could not understand it, and she wished that she knew more about her Master's past.

Suddenly Anakin stopped without warning. The next moment, Ahsoka felt it too – a strange disturbance in the Force.

"We're not alone," she said, feeling nervous.

"It's the dark side of the Force," Anakin told her.

Rotta hid himself under the flap of the rucksack, squeaking in fear.

"Whatever it is, it's coming for Rotta," said Anakin. "Time to split up."

"We'll face it together, Master," Ahsoka replied, sounding braver than she felt.

"Not this time, Snips," Anakin insisted. "I have a far more important mission for you."

"More important than keeping you alive?" his Padawan enquired.

"Ahsoka, I need you to trust me on this one," said Anakin. "Now, here's the plan . . ."

The sentry droid took Padmé's blaster and hologram projector and dropped them on the floor. She was roughly pushed into a cell and then the droid faced the cell door and aimed its blaster at her, ready to fire if she tried to escape. There were another four battle droids nearby, and Padmé knew that she didn't have a chance. Then, as if in answer to her predicament, her holoprojector began to flash and buzz. Someone was trying to get hold of her. Padmé thought fast – this could be her only chance to live!

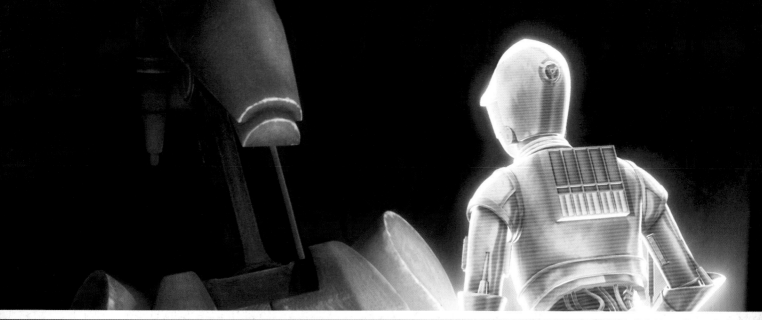

"What's that?" asked a battle droid.

"Don't touch that!" Padmé said. "Whatever you do, keep away from that. Please, I beg you!"

She felt sure that this would make them curious enough to touch it. Sure enough, one of the droids fell into her trap. He picked up the holoprojector, which answered the call. A holographic image of C-3PO flickered in front of them.

"At last you answered!" he cried. "Oh, I've been so worried." Then he noticed the battle droid. "Wait, who are you? You're not Mistress Padmé!"

"Threepio, get help!" Padmé yelled at the top of her voice. "I'm being held by Ziro the Hutt!"

"You're in trouble!" 3PO exclaimed. "I knew it!"

The droid threw down the holoprojector and crushed it with his foot, but the damage had been done. Padmé just had to hope that 3PO had heard the message, and that he would send help before it was too late.

Meanwhile, Anakin was walking across the dark Tatooine desert, carrying Rotta's heavy rucksack on his back. A hooded figure zoomed towards him on a speeder bike, and Anakin stopped and looked up. It was Count Dooku. The Sith Lord got off the bike and strode towards Anakin, looking evil and dangerous. Anakin turned his lightsaber on.

"Surrender the Huttlet or die, Skywalker," Dooku told him.

Sith lightning erupted from his fingertips as he attacked Anakin. The young Jedi used his lightsaber to protect himself. Then Dooku took out his own lightsaber and they began to battle.

"Your training has come a long way, boy," said Dooku.

Anakin continued to duel, not allowing Dooku's words to distract him.

"Ah, now I remember," Dooku went on. "This was your home planet, wasn't it? I sense strong feelings. Feelings of pain. Loss."

Anakin knew that he had to stay focused. He used the Force to send a whirl of sand swirling around Dooku, but after a moment Dooku sent the sand whizzing back towards Anakin. Then he used his blade to slash Anakin's rucksack in half.

"You've failed, Jedi," he said with a wicked grin of triumph. "I have just killed Jabba's son."

"You've fallen for my little trick, Count," Anakin told him.

He took off the rucksack and a number of rocks fell out on to the sand.

"The Huttlet is with my Padawan, safely at Jabba's palace," Anakin went on.

"My web is strong enough to catch your little Padawan," sneered Dooku.

"She's more powerful than you think," Anakin retorted.

Ahsoka was steadily making her way towards Jabba's palace. Rotta was safely on her back, and R2 was close behind her. But just as she was thinking that she had almost completed her mission, her senses told her to be alert. She ignited her lightsaber just seconds before three MagnaGuards leaped out of hiding, ready to attack. They were carrying attack staffs, which crackled and fizzed with deadly energy. Ahsoka was in serious trouble!

Dooku took out a holoprojector. "Look, I have a message from your Padawan," he said with a nasty smile.

A blue hologram showed an image of Ahsoka battling the three MagnaGuards.

"After my droids kill Jabba's son, they will deliver your Padawan to him for punishment," Dooku said.

Anakin would have liked to battle Count Dooku, but he knew that it was far more important to reach Ahsoka and help her. With super-fast Jedi reflexes, he leaped into the air, landed on Dooku's speeder and raced off into the desert before the Sith Lord could stop him.

Padmé was taken into the throne room to stand in front of Ziro the Hutt.

"You tried to call for help, Senator," Ziro said. "You are too dangerous to be kept alive!"

Padmé did not flinch as the sentry droids pointed their blasters at her.

"Killing a Galactic Senator, here on Coruscant?" she said. "Are you out of your mind?"

Suddenly an explosion echoed through the palace. Republic shock troopers charged into the room. C-3PO had got the message and Padmé was saved! Ziro tried to slither away, but it was too late. In seconds he was surrounded by armed clone troopers.

"I had no choice!" Ziro babbled. "Dooku said he'd kill me if I didn't help him kidnap Jabba's son. You have to believe me. I love that Huttlet!"

Padmé gave a smile of relief. Now that she had Ziro where she wanted him, she felt sure that she could save her husband.

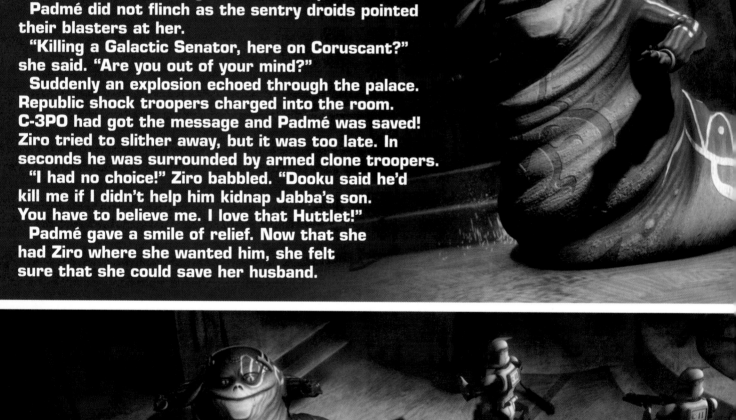

Ahsoka was outnumbered by the vicious MagnaGuards. R2 tried to help with his little buzz saw, but he was clubbed down.

"Artoo!" Ahsoka yelled. "Three against two . . . Stinky, you watch my back."

Ahsoka used all her Jedi skills to keep out of the way of the slashing staffs. She leaped back on to a small sand dune. One of the MagnaGuards grazed her arm with his staff and she almost cried out as the electricity burned her. Then she sent the guard flying backwards with a blow from her lightsaber. Another MagnaGuard tried to hit Rotta on the head, and Ahsoka protected the baby Hutt with her own body, taking another blow on her arm. At last she gained an advantage and managed to destroy one of the guards, cutting it in half.

At that moment, Ahsoka heard an engine high above her. When she looked up, she saw Anakin on a speeder bike. He was racing at top speed, and he didn't see her or the MagnaGuards.

"Master!" she yelled. "Over here!"

But Anakin was already out of hearing range and racing towards the castle. Ahsoka sighed and turned back to the two MagnaGuards who were still attacking her.

"You are going back to Dooku in pieces!" she told them.

As Ahsoka was defending herself against her attackers, Anakin raced into Jabba's castle. TC-70 appeared in front of him.

"Where is my Padawan?" asked Anakin.

"This way," the droid replied. "Your weapon, please."

Anakin gave the droid his lightsaber and was taken to the throne room.

"This is Jedi Knight Anakin Skywalker," TC-70 said. "As Count Dooku said, your son is not with him."

"Your son's not here?" Anakin exclaimed.

He worried about where Ahsoka could be as Jabba glowered down at him, roaring accusations. Clearly, something had gone very wrong. Anakin used the Force to draw his lightsaber from TC-70's hands into his. He ignited it and pressed the blade against Jabba's throat.

"What have you done with my Padawan?" he demanded.

"You came here to kill Jabba," cried TC-70.

"Mighty Jabba, I came here to negotiate," Anakin said.

"You came here to die," the protocol droid said, translating Jabba's words.

Anakin was surrounded by guards, all ready to fire on the Jedi.

"Stop!" cried Ahsoka's voice.

A hsoka strode in with Rotta in her arms.
"Most patient Jabba, your son has arrived alive and well,"
Anakin said, lowering his lightsaber.

Jabba gazed at the boy with love and relief and then looked up at the Jedi.

"NOBATA! KEELYA JEDI!" he roared.

His tone of voice did not sound grateful or apologetic.

"You are to be executed immediately," TC-70 translated.

Ahsoka and Anakin stared at each other and then ignited their lightsabers.

"Does this always happen to you?" asked Ahsoka.

"Everywhere I go," Anakin replied.

Rotta began to sob, and then Jabba's holoprojector beeped.

"Your uncle Ziro is contacting us," TC-70 reported.

However, when the holoprojector was answered, it was Padmé's image that appeared.

"Greetings, honourable Jabba," said Padmé. "I am Senator Amidala of the Galactic Senate. I have discovered a plot against you by one of your own."

She explained the evil Sith plot, and then Ziro appeared and admitted everything. Jabba roared in fury.

"Perhaps you will allow the Republic to use your trade routes and hostilities can come to an end," Padmé suggested.

Jabba thought for a moment. Then he gave a deep laugh and spoke to Ahsoka and Anakin.

"Jabba agrees," translated the protocol droid. "A treaty is in order."

"You will not regret this, Jabba," said Padmé.

Ahsoka and Anakin smiled in tired relief and then bowed to Jabba.

"Jabba would be most appreciative if you bring Dooku to justice for his crimes against the Hutts," said TC-70.

"You can count on it, Jabba," Anakin promised.

Ahsoka and Anakin shared a warm smile. Ahsoka felt a sudden rush of confidence in herself. For years it had been her dream to become a Jedi Knight. Finally, she had taken part in a real Jedi mission . . . and she had succeeded! At last her dream was within reach.

TRADING CARDS

You can make your own *Clone Wars* trading cards. Use them to decorate your bedroom wall, play with your friends or memorise all the important statistics.

YOU WILL NEED:

WHITE CARD
SCISSORS
COLOURED PENS, CRAYONS OR PENCILS.
BLACK PEN

1) Copy the trading card template on to a piece of white card and cut it out (ask a grown-up to give you a hand).

2) Decide which character is going to be on your card and draw a picture of them in the space at the top of the card. Be as accurate as you can!

3) From the list of statistics, fill in the information on your card with a black pen. You can choose what information to include (some suggestions are below). Then give the character a power rating by colouring in the stars. (The weakest is 1 star and the strongest is 5 stars.)

Name.............................
Species ....
Affiliation ....
Height ....
Weight..........................
Weapon ....
Vehicle ....

4) Repeat these steps until you have as many cards as you want. Now make some for your friends!

Ahsoka Tano
SPECIES: Togruta
AFFILIATION: Jedi
HEIGHT: 1.61m
WEAPON: Lightsaber

Anakin Skywalker
SPECIES: Human
HEIGHT: 1.85m
WEAPON: Lightsaber
VEHICLE: N-1 starfighter, hotrod speeder, custom modified Jedi starfighter
AFFILIATION: Jedi

Asajj Ventress
SPECIES: Rattataki
AFFILIATION: Confederacy of Independent Systems
WEAPON: Paired lightsabers
VEHICLE: Geonosian fanblade starfighter

Clone Captain Rex (CC-7567)
SPECIES: Human
AFFILIATION: Clone trooper, 501st Legion
HEIGHT: 1.83m
WEAPON: Blaster pistols, blaster rifle
VEHICLE: Republic gunship

Count Dooku
SPECIES: Human
HEIGHT: 1.93m
WEAPON: Lightsaber
VEHICLE: Geonosian speeder, Geonosian solar sailer
AFFILIATION: Sith, Confederacy of Independent Systems

Jabba the Hutt
SPECIES: Hutt
HEIGHT: 3.9m long
WEAPON: Assassins and bounty hunters
VEHICLE: Ubrikkian luxury sail barge, repulsor sled
Affiliation: Criminal

Obi-Wan Kenobi
SPECIES: Human
HEIGHT: 1.79m
WEAPON: Lightsaber
VEHICLE: Jedi starfighter
AFFILIATION: Jedi

Padmé Amidala
SPECIES: Human
HEIGHT: 1.65m
WEAPON: Royal pistol
VEHICLE: Naboo Royal (Queen's) Starship, Naboo Royal Cruiser, Naboo yacht, Naboo star skiff
AFFILIATION: Galactic Senate

Supreme Chancellor Palpatine
SPECIES: Human
HEIGHT: 1.73m
WEAPON: Dark side lightning
VEHICLE: Imperial shuttle
AFFILIATION: Galactic Senate, Galactic Republic, Sith

Yoda
SPECIES: Unknown
HEIGHT: 0.66m
WEAPON: Lightsaber
AFFILIATION: Jedi

NAME:
....
....

POWER RATING:
☆☆☆☆☆

....
....
....
....
....

TEMPLATE ▶

Answers

Page 16 - MISSING WORDS

1) Asajj Ventress's fanblade starfighter, *Last Call*, is equipped with a **gemcutter** and **tractor beams.**

2) Anakin's starfighter began as a standard Delta-7 *Aethersprite* that he has customised to suit his need for **speed** and control. It has four **laser cannons** on each wingtip and a **proton torpedo launcher** along the ship's dorsal centre line.

3) Jabba's the Hutt's luxury yacht ship has hidden **gunports** as an unpleasant surprise for would-be pirates.

4) Asajj Ventress uses twin curved, red bladed **lightsabers.** The handles can connect to form a S-shaped, double-bladed weapon.

5) Each lightsaber is handcrafted as part of a Jedi's training and may have unique design elements. A lightsaber's **energy blade** is produced by several **crystals** connected to a power source within the lightsaber's handle.

6) Blasters fire beams of intense **light energy** and the colour of the energy bolts varies. A blaster's gas chamber carries enough blaster gas for over **500** shots. Stun blasts knock the target out for up to **ten** minutes, while a **full power blast** can penetrate **armour.**

7) Jedi are not allowed to **marry.**

8) Ahsoka's **astromech droid** is called R3-G7.

9) Asajj gave Anakin his **scar** during a **duel** on Coruscant.

10) Anakin Skywalker has earned the title "**hero** with no fear" for his exploits in battle.

Page 17 - PUZZLE PAGE

Riddles
1) A stamp
2) A penny
3) A secret

Anagrams
1) Master Yoda
2) Padmé Amidala
3) Palpatine

Conundrums
The Tusken Raider's bantha is called Tuesday.
The Padawan goes to bed while it is still light